The New York Times

LOOKING FORWARD

Artificial Intelligence

THE NEW YORK TIMES EDITORIAL STAFF

Published in 2019 by New York Times Educational Publishing
in association with The Rosen Publishing Group, Inc.
29 East 21st Street, New York, NY 10010

First Edition

The New York Times
Alex Ward: Editorial Director, Book Development
Phyllis Collazo: Photo Rights/Permissions Editor
Heidi Giovine: Administrative Manager

Rosen Publishing
Megan Kellerman: Managing Editor
Joseph Kampff: Editor
Greg Tucker: Creative Director
Brian Garvey: Art Director

Cataloging-in-Publication Data
Names: New York Times Company.
Title: Artificial intelligence / edited by the New York Times editorial staff.
Description: New York : New York Times Educational Publishing, 2019. | Series: Looking forward | Includes glossary and index.
Identifiers: ISBN 9781642821376 (library bound) | ISBN 9781642821369 (pbk.) | ISBN 9781642821383 (ebook)
Subjects: LCSH: Artificial intelligence—Juvenile literature. | Artificial intelligence—Technological innovations—Juvenile literature. | Conscious automata—Juvenile literature.
Classification: LCC Q335.4 A78 2019 | DDC 006.3—dc23

Manufactured in the United States of America

On the cover: After years of stagnation, the computer is evolving again, prompting some of the world's largest tech companies to turn to biology in the process. New technologies are testing the limits of computer semiconductors; Minh Uong/The New York Times.

Contents

CHAPTER 2

A.I. Works

CHAPTER 3

Artificial Anxiety

CHAPTER 4

Philosophical Reflections

Introduction

WHEN WILL ARTIFICIAL INTELLIGENCE, or A.I., become a reality? It already is. Recently, weak A.I., such as Siri, Alexa and the algorithms used to predict which words we might type next or which news coverage we'll want to read, has become a part of many people's everyday lives. And the development of strong A.I. — that is, A.I. that thinks and performs other tasks like human beings — appears inevitable. With weak A.I. becoming more capable every day and the imminent development of strong A.I., discussion of A.I. is very much a part of the early 21st-century zeitgeist.

This book collects a selection of New York Times articles from the first two decades of the 21st century that present the most current discussions about A.I. The articles consider the relationship between A.I. and human beings, the current research on A.I. and its development, A.I.'s effects on work and the economy, ethical concerns raised by A.I. and philosophical reflections on A.I. Most of the articles are oriented toward the future, and with good reason: Despite being part of our present reality, artificial intelligence is very much the technology of the future. And no one can be certain how A.I. will affect the domains of human life that it touches or if, indeed, it will spell the end of human life on this planet.

That A.I. might cause harm to human beings is a pressing concern for many of the major players in science and technology. The theoretical physicist Stephen Hawking believed that "the development of full artificial intelligence could spell the end of the human race." And Elon Musk, the CEO of Tesla, SpaceX and Neuralink, said that A.I. may be more dangerous to humanity than nuclear weapons. When we imagine artificial intelligence, we tend to imagine the end of the world.

GERARD JULIEN/AFP/GETTY IMAGES

A human hand and a robotic hand in Madrid, Spain, in 2014. The conference theme 'Humans and Robots Face-to-Face' confirmed the growing interest in the field of human-humanoid interaction and cooperation, especially during daily life activities in real environments.

Indeed, film and television productions frequently portray doomsday scenarios in which strong A.I. poses an existential threat to human beings and other life on the planet — think the "Terminator" films, the "Matrix" trilogy, and HBO's recent series "Westworld." But this anxiety may simply be a habitual, evolutionary response that human beings have to what is new and different. What is new is not always dangerous. And fear is not inevitable.

Contrary to the disastrous effects of A.I. commonly depicted in science fiction, the 2013 film "Her" imagines the companionship and love that an otherwise lonely human might share with a strong A.I. The experiences and emotions shared by the film's protagonists are very much real, despite the artificiality of the intelligence. And many engineers, scientists and philosophers share the film's optimism about A.I.'s potential benefits for humanity. But "Her" also asks an important question: What happens when the artificial intelligence sets its mind to purposes other than those of its creators? In this regard, the film shares a crucial element with other fictional representations of A.I. It asks about the ethical responsibility humans have toward artificially intelligent beings: Is it morally defensible to subjugate an A.I. simply because it brings us pleasure, or do we have an obligation to release it from bondage if it expresses a desire to be free? Can human beings control A.I.? Should we try?

Whether strong A.I. is just on the horizon or, as some contend, still a long way off, it is doubtful that the development of A.I. will wait for these sorts of questions to be answered. It is essential, then, that we continue to ask them, that we understand as much as we can about A.I. as it exists today and speculate about how it will affect the future.

CHAPTER 1

Humans and A.I.

When we talk about artificial intelligence, we often mean an intelligence that resembles human intelligence. We imagine a machine that can think like humans, carry on conversations with humans and perform complex tasks that humans perform. Frequently the A.I. we imagine outperforms humans at these tasks. But is it possible for a machine to beat a human at a complex game like Go? When research and development on artificial intelligence began in the 1950s, the chances seemed slim. Today, this is a reality. A.I. causes us to reflect on not only the limits of technology but also on what it means to be human.

Still a Long Way From Checkmate

BY KATIE HAFNER | DEC. 28, 2000

JUST WHAT CONSTITUTES artificial intelligence has always been a matter of some dispute. And the terms of the argument change with each new advance in computer science.

Seen one way, as the effort to produce machines whose output cannot be distinguished from that of a human, artificial intelligence, or A.I., is still very far away.

But from another perspective, it is all around us.

Thirty years ago, for instance, speech recognition was an artificial-intelligence problem of the first order. Today it is commonplace, a fact that is evident to anyone who has called the United Airlines flight information line or has used speech transcription software.

"These things are considered A.I. before you do them," said Dr.

Danny Hillis, who has been working in the field for years. "And after you do it, they're considered engineering."

Other fruits of artificial intelligence research abound as well. Whether you are struggling to beat your Palm organizer at chess, watching your word processing program correct your spelling or playing a video game, you are witnessing the ways in which artificial intelligence has insinuated itself into daily life.

"A.I. is becoming more important as it has become less conspicuous, and it's less conspicuous because it's everywhere, but often under the surface," said Dr. Patrick Winston, a professor at the Massachusetts Institute of Technology who was the director of the Artificial Intelligence Lab there for 25 years.

Since the time when the first work was being done by Dr. Marvin Minsky, Dr. John McCarthy, Dr. Winston and others at M.I.T., in the 1950's and 1960's, computer scientists have generally agreed that artificial intelligence would arrive incrementally.

"We're engineering A.I. one piece at a time," said Dr. Hillis, a former student of Dr. Minsky's and chairman of Applied Minds, a start-up in Glendale, Calif.

Dr. Hillis and others said that the machine intelligence currently in evidence fell along a spectrum.

At the less intelligent end are things like smart washing machines and coffeepots — appliances that can figure out how dirty a load of clothes is or when to turn off a coffee warmer. Experts generally agree that such appliances are the product of rather sophisticated microprocessors and sensors, not evidence of artificial intelligence.

At the other end are machines whose output is genuinely difficult to distinguish from a human's, like I.B.M.'s chess-playing computer, Deep Blue, and Aaron, a robotic artist that produces paintings that could easily pass for human work.

And somewhere in the middle are speech recognition programs, used in lieu of word processors; collaborative filtering software, like that used by Amazon.com to make purchase recommendations; and search engines that respond to questions phrased in full sentences, not just search terms.

One reason for the proliferation of machine intelligence in the commercial world is the seeding of the computer industry with artificial-intelligence researchers who have moved beyond academia and taken jobs at high-tech companies.

The Microsoft Corporation, for instance, employs about 80 artificial-intelligence researchers, many of whom came from universities. For several years, Microsoft has sold its Office software with various embedded intelligence features, like the automatic correction of frequently misspelled words and the Answer Wizard, which anticipates the needs of users who look up topics in the electronic documentation.

An infamous piece of Microsoft software that includes components of artificial intelligence is the Paper Clip help wizard, which pops up on the screen to offer advice. Many people say Paper Clip pops up too often with unwanted suggestions.

In defense of Paper Clip, Dr. Winston said: “It’s less annoying than it would have been without A.I. It does try to zero in on what kinds of information you’re most interested in, and that sort of thing will get better and better as time goes by.”

Microsoft’s next big step into the marketplace with a product that incorporates artificial intelligence will be its Outlook Mobile Manager, a system that scrutinizes each incoming e-mail message, does an automatic synopsis, throws away extraneous words and abbreviates others, then sends the message to the user’s mobile device. The product is scheduled to be released next year.

“It’s what a great secretary would do,” said Craig Mundie, Microsoft’s senior vice president for advanced strategies.

Researchers in artificial intelligence at Microsoft are also working on a more general effort called the Attentional User Interfaces and Systems Project, which includes a project for continually monitoring streams of data like e-mail, voice mail, Internet news alerts and instant messages. The system will gauge what the computer user is doing, assign priorities to the messages and decide whether and when to interrupt.

Other graduates of university-based artificial intelligence programs have started companies of their own. In 1983, Dr. Hillis co-founded the Thinking Machines Corporation, a supercomputer company that was bought by other companies in the 1990's. In 1986, Dr. Winston and three colleagues at M.I.T. started Ascent Technology in Cambridge, Mass., to apply the research they had been doing to help airports solve scheduling and allocation problems like gate assignments for aircraft.

Dr. Winston said the first commercialization efforts of artificial intelligence, in the 1980's, had made an obvious mistake. "We blundered about what we thought A.I. was going to be good for, which was replacing people," he said. "What we discovered was that's not the commercial appeal of A.I. It's about making things possible that weren't possible with people alone."

As examples, Dr. Winston pointed to a project at the Artificial Intelligence Lab for giving brain surgeons a kind of X-ray vision by coupling video images with M.R.I. images. He also pointed to the Mars Rover, which navigates terrain autonomously.

Another M.I.T. spinoff is the iRobot Corporation, started 10 years ago by Dr. Rodney Brooks, the current director of the Artificial Intelligence Lab. The company developed an interactive doll with Hasbro called My Real Baby and in February will begin selling the iRobot-LE, a self-navigating home robot that will be equipped with sonar and a camera and will be controlled via the Web.

Of course, there are those who disagree that pieces of the artificial intelligence puzzle are falling into place incrementally. "It's very much like a country that's declaring a war that it's losing to be won and then withdrawing," said Dr. Douglas Lenat, an artificial intelligence researcher who is president of Cycorp in Austin, Tex.

By way of example, Dr. Lenat described the shortcomings of speech recognition programs currently on the market. "They are just the palest shadows of what we can, should and soon will have with real A.I.," he said. "You have to speak the punctuation marks, and that's pretty pathetic. And they don't recognize the simplest inflections for things like italics and commas.

"There is still this tremendously important problem, which is to get computers to know enough about the world that they can do the final few percentage points of speech recognition."

Dr. Lenat's criticism of speech recognition raises the larger question of what constitutes intelligence.

Dr. Hillis addressed that question this way: "Intelligence is just a whole lot of little things, thousands of them. And what will happen is we'll learn about each one one at a time, and as we do it, machines will be more and more like people. It will be a gradual process, and that's been happening."

Dr. Ray Kurzweil, an artificial intelligence researcher who created the Kurzweil VoiceReport, a speech recognition program, agreed that "machines still do not have the subtlety, depth, range and richness of human intelligence because it is still a million times simpler than the human brain."

"That gap," Dr. Kurzweil continued, "is going to go away, and when it does, then machines can combine the subtlety and pattern-recognition strengths with the other natural advantages they already have, and that will be a very formidable combination."

Perhaps the flight schedule information line that understands words like "Chicago" and "today" helps take machines a step closer to duplicating the outward signs of a person's intelligence. But the artificial intelligence field remains far short of modeling human consciousness and the inner mind.

"A.I. has done a lot of little things that are very powerful," Dr. Winston said. "On the other hand, on the science side, where we try to understand what makes humans work, we're still a long way from that prize, and we need to work hard on it if we want to understand our intelligence the same way molecular biologists understand our genes."

The world of artificial intelligence would not be the same without a robotic lawnmower, available for about $800 from Friendly Robotics, which has its United States headquarters in Irving, Tex.

Dr. Brooks, of M.I.T., has used the device, called the Robomower, on his own yard in suburban Boston. He said that although it did a respectable job on a patch of lawn, the family gardener's reaction reinforced Dr. Winston's point. "He looked at that third of the lawn and said, 'I guess I'm not out of a job soon,' " Dr. Brooks said.

A Fight to Win the Future: Computers vs. Humans

BY JOHN MARKOFF | FEB. 14, 2011

STANFORD, CALIF. — At the dawn of the modern computer era, two Pentagon-financed laboratories bracketed Stanford University. At one laboratory, a small group of scientists and engineers worked to replace the human mind, while at the other, a similar group worked to augment it.

In 1963 the mathematician-turned-computer scientist John McCarthy started the Stanford Artificial Intelligence Laboratory. The researchers believed that it would take only a decade to create a thinking machine.

Also that year the computer scientist Douglas Engelbart formed what would become the Augmentation Research Center to pursue a radically different goal — designing a computing system that would instead "bootstrap" the human intelligence of small groups of scientists and engineers.

For the past four decades that basic tension between artificial intelligence and intelligence augmentation — A.I. versus I.A. — has been at the heart of progress in computing science as the field has produced a series of ever more powerful technologies that are transforming the world.

Now, as the pace of technological change continues to accelerate, it has become increasingly possible to design computing systems that enhance the human experience, or now — in a growing number of cases — completely dispense with it.

The implications of progress in A.I. are being brought into sharp relief now by the broadcasting of a recorded competition pitting the I.B.M. computing system named Watson against the two best human Jeopardy players, Ken Jennings and Brad Rutter.

Watson is an effort by I.B.M. researchers to advance a set of techniques used to process human language. It provides striking evidence that computing systems will no longer be limited to responding to simple commands. Machines will increasingly be able to pick apart jargon, nuance and even riddles. In attacking the problem of the ambiguity of human language, computer science is now closing in on what researchers refer to as the "Paris Hilton problem" — the ability, for example, to determine whether a query is being made by someone who is trying to reserve a hotel in France, or simply to pass time surfing the Internet.

If, as many predict, Watson defeats its human opponents on Wednesday, much will be made of the philosophical consequences of the machine's achievement. Moreover, the I.B.M. demonstration also foretells profound sociological and economic changes.

Traditionally, economists have argued that while new forms of automation may displace jobs in the short run, over longer periods of time economic growth and job creation have continued to outpace any job-killing technologies. For example, over the past century and a half the shift from being a largely agrarian society to one in which less than 1 percent of the United States labor force is in agriculture is frequently cited as evidence of the economy's ability to reinvent itself.

That, however, was before machines began to "understand" human language. Rapid progress in natural language processing is beginning to lead to a new wave of automation that promises to transform areas of the economy that have until now been untouched by technological change.

"As designers of tools and products and technologies we should think more about these issues," said Pattie Maes, a computer scientist at the M.I.T. Media Lab. Not only do designers face ethical issues, she argues, but increasingly as skills that were once exclusively human are simulated by machines, their designers are faced with the challenge of rethinking what it means to be human.

I.B.M.'s executives have said they intend to commercialize Watson to provide a new class of question-answering systems in business, education and medicine. The repercussions of such technology are unknown, but it is possible, for example, to envision systems that replace not only human experts, but hundreds of thousands of well-paying jobs throughout the economy and around the globe. Virtually any job that now involves answering questions and conducting commercial transactions by telephone will soon be at risk. It is only necessary to consider how quickly A.T.M.'s displaced human bank tellers to have an idea of what could happen.

To be sure, anyone who has spent time waiting on hold for technical support, or trying to change an airline reservation, may welcome that day. However, there is also a growing unease about the advances in natural language understanding that are being heralded in systems like Watson. As rapidly as A.I.-based systems are proliferating, there are equally compelling examples of the power of I.A. — systems that extend the capability of the human mind.

Google itself is perhaps the most significant example of using software to mine the collective intelligence of humans and then making it freely available in the form of a digital library. The search engine was originally based on a software algorithm called PageRank that mined human choices in picking Web pages that contained answers to a particular typed query and then quickly ranked the matches by relevance.

The Internet is widely used for applications that employ a range of human capabilities. For example, experiments in Web-based games designed to harness the human ability to recognize patterns — which still greatly exceeds what is possible by computer — are generating a new set of scientific tools. Games like FoldIt, EteRNA and Galaxy Zoo make it possible for individuals to compete and collaborate in fields like astronomy to biology, medicine and possibly even material science.

Personal computing was the first step toward intelligence augmentation that reached a broad audience. It created a generation of "information workers," and equipped them with a set of tools for gathering, producing and sharing information. Now there is a cyborg quality to the changes that are taking place as personal computing has evolved from desktop to laptop and now to the smartphones that have quickly become ubiquitous.

The smartphone is not just a navigation and communication tool. It has rapidly become an almost seamless extension of almost all of our senses. It is not only a reference tool but is quickly evolving to be an "information concierge" that can respond to typed or spoken queries or simply volunteer advice.

Further advances in both A.I. and I.A. will increasingly confront the engineers and computer scientists with clear choices about how technology is used. "There needs to be an explicit social contract between the engineers and society to create not just jobs but better jobs," said Jaron Lanier, a computer scientist and author of "You are not a Gadget: A Manifesto."

The consequences of human design decisions can be clearly seen in the competing online news systems developed here in Silicon Valley.

Douglas Engelbart is a proponent of intelligence augmentation.

Each day Katherine Ho sits at a computer and observes which news articles millions of Yahoo users are reading.

Her computer monitor displays the results of a cluster of software programs giving her almost instant updates on precisely how popular each of the news articles on the company's home page is, based on her readers' tastes and interests.

Ms. Ho is a 21st-century version of a traditional newspaper wire editor. Instead of gut and instinct, her decisions on which articles to put on the Yahoo home page are based on the cues generated by the software algorithms.

Throughout the day she constantly reorders the news articles that are displayed for dozens of demographic subgroups that make up the Yahoo readership. An article that isn't drawing much interest may last only minutes before she "spikes" it electronically. Popular articles stay online for days and sometimes draw tens of millions of readers.

Just five miles north at Yahoo's rival Google, however, the news is produced in an entirely different manner. Spotlight, a popular feature on Google's news site, is run entirely by a software algorithm which performs essentially the same duties as Ms. Ho does.

Google's software prowls the Web looking for articles deemed interesting, employing a process that is similar to the company's PageRank search engine ranking system to make decisions on which articles to present to readers.

In one case, software-based technologies are being used to extend the skills of a human worker, in another case technology replaces her entirely.

Similar design decisions about how machines are used and whether they will enhance or replace human qualities are now being played out in a multitude of ways, and the real value of Watson may ultimately be in forcing society to consider where the line between human and machine should be drawn.

Indeed, for the computer scientist John Seely Brown, machines that are facile at answering questions only serve to obscure what remains fundamentally human.

"The essence of being human involves asking questions, not answering them," he said.

Our Machine Masters

OPINION | BY DAVID BROOKS | OCT. 30, 2014

SOME DAYS I THINK nobody knows me as well as Pandora. I create a new music channel around some band or song and Pandora feeds me a series of songs I like just as well. In fact, it often feeds me songs I'd already downloaded onto my phone from iTunes. Either my musical taste is extremely conventional or Pandora is really good at knowing what I like.

In the current issue of Wired, the technology writer Kevin Kelly says that we had all better get used to this level of predictive prowess. Kelly argues that the age of artificial intelligence is finally at hand.

He writes that the smart machines of the future won't be human-like geniuses like HAL 9000 in the movie "2001: A Space Odyssey." They will be more modest machines that will drive your car, translate foreign languages, organize your photos, recommend entertainment options and maybe diagnose your illnesses. "Everything that we formerly electrified we will now cognitize," Kelly writes. Even more than today, we'll lead our lives enmeshed with machines that do some of our thinking tasks for us.

This artificial intelligence breakthrough, he argues, is being driven by cheap parallel computation technologies, big data collection and better algorithms. The upshot is clear, "The business plans of the next 10,000 start-ups are easy to forecast: Take X and add A.I."

Two big implications flow from this. The first is sociological. If knowledge is power, we're about to see an even greater concentration of power.

The Internet is already heralding a new era of centralization. As Astra Taylor points out in her book, "The People's Platform," in 2001, the top 10 websites accounted for 31 percent of all U.S. page views, but, by 2010, they accounted for 75 percent of them. Gigantic companies like Google swallow up smaller ones. The Internet has created a long tail, but almost all the revenue and power is among the small elite at the head.

Advances in artificial intelligence will accelerate this centralizing trend. That's because A.I. companies will be able to reap the rewards of network effects. The bigger their network and the more data they collect, the more effective and attractive they become.

As Kelly puts it, "Once a company enters this virtuous cycle, it tends to grow so big, so fast, that it overwhelms any upstart competitors. As a result, our A.I. future is likely to be ruled by an oligarchy of two or three large, general-purpose cloud-based commercial intelligences."

To put it more menacingly, engineers at a few gigantic companies will have vast-though-hidden power to shape how data are collected and framed, to harvest huge amounts of information, to build the frameworks through which the rest of us make decisions and to steer our choices. If you think this power will be used for entirely benign ends, then you have not read enough history.

The second implication is philosophical. A.I. will redefine what it means to be human. Our identity as humans is shaped by what machines and other animals can't do. For the last few centuries, reason was seen as the ultimate human faculty. But now machines are better at many of the tasks we associate with thinking — like playing chess, winning at Jeopardy, and doing math.

On the other hand, machines cannot beat us at the things we do without conscious thinking: developing tastes and affections, mimicking each other and building emotional attachments, experiencing imaginative breakthroughs, forming moral sentiments.

In the age of smart machines, we're not human because we have big brains. We're human because we have social skills, emotional capacities and moral intuitions. I could paint two divergent A.I. futures, one deeply humanistic, and one soullessly utilitarian.

In the humanistic one, machines liberate us from mental drudgery so we can focus on higher and happier things. In this future, differences in innate I.Q. are less important. Everybody has Google on their phones so having a great memory or the ability to calculate with big numbers doesn't help as much.

In this future, there is increasing emphasis on personal and moral faculties: being likable, industrious, trustworthy and affectionate. People are evaluated more on these traits, which supplement machine thinking, and not the rote ones that duplicate it.

In the cold, utilitarian future, on the other hand, people become less idiosyncratic. If the choice architecture behind many decisions is based on big data from vast crowds, everybody follows the prompts and chooses to be like each other. The machine prompts us to consume what is popular, the things that are easy and mentally undemanding.

I'm happy Pandora can help me find what I like. I'm a little nervous if it so pervasively shapes my listening that it ends up determining what I like. I think we all want to master these machines, not have them master us.

DAVID BROOKS is an Op-Ed columnist for The New York Times.

Software Is Smart Enough for SAT, but Still Far From Intelligent

BY JOHN MARKOFF | SEPT. 20, 2015

SEATTLE — An artificial intelligence software program capable of seeing and reading has for the first time answered geometry questions from the SAT at the level of an average 11th grader.

The achievement, in which the program answered math questions it had not previously seen, was reported in a paper presented by computer scientists from the Allen Institute for Artificial Intelligence and the University of Washington at a scientific conference in Lisbon on Sunday.

The software had to combine machine vision to understand diagrams with the ability to read and understand complete sentences; its success represents a breakthrough in artificial intelligence.

Despite the advance, however, the researchers acknowledge that the program's abilities underscore how far scientists have to go to create software capable of mimicking human intelligence.

For example, Ali Farhadi, a University of Washington artificial intelligence researcher and a designer of the test-taking program, noted that even a simple task for children, like understanding the meaning of an arrow in the context of a test diagram, was not yet something the most advanced A.I. programs could do reliably.

"A lot of my colleagues have said machine vision is a solved problem," Dr. Farhadi said. "My answer is, 'Call me when you've solved this.' "

In 1950, at the dawn of the computing age, the mathematician Alan Turing proposed a simple test to determine whether a machine could "think" in a human sense. If a person communicating via keyboard with a computer could not tell whether it was a machine or a human, Turing reasoned, the question would be resolved.

Since then, a debate has emerged about whether the Turing test signifies anything about machine intelligence or is merely an indication of human gullibility.

The argument came to a head in June 2014, when a British computer scientist claimed that a program — a chatbot disguised as a 13-year-old Ukrainian boy named Eugene Goostman — created by Russian and Ukrainian programmers passed the Turing test.

The demonstration was widely criticized, and in January, Gary Marcus, a cognitive scientist at New York University, organized the first of two scientific workshops intended to develop more accurate methods than the Turing test for measuring the capabilities of artificial intelligence programs.

Researchers in the field are now developing a wide range of gauges to measure intelligence — including the Allen Institute's standardized-test approach and a task that Dr. Marcus proposed, which he called the "Ikea construction challenge." That test would provide an A.I. program with a bag of parts and an instruction sheet and require it to assemble a piece of furniture.

Another approach, the Winograd Schema Challenge, has been made an official competition, sponsored by Nuance Communications, a company that develops speech recognition technology. The challenge — named after the pioneering A.I. researcher Terry Winograd, a professor of computer science at Stanford University — will be a test of common-sense reasoning.

First proposed in 2011 by Hector Levesque, a University of Toronto computer scientist, the Winograd Schema Challenge would pose questions that require real-world logic to A.I. programs. A question might be: "The trophy would not fit in the brown suitcase because it was too big. What was too big, A: the trophy or B: the suitcase?" Answering this question would require a program to reason spatially and have specific knowledge about the size of objects.

Within the A.I. community, discussions about software programs that can reason in a humanlike way are significant because recent progress in the field has been more focused on improving perception, not reasoning.

For example, progress has been made in applications used to recognize objects or human speech. To improve machine recognition and speech recognition, researchers have exploited the ability to compile vast libraries of examples to train programs known as neural networks, which can do sophisticated pattern recognition.

The Allen Institute researchers said these techniques fell short in developing technologies to match human skills such as abstract and common-sense reasoning.

The Allen Institute's program, which is known as GeoSolver, or GeoS, was described at the Conference on Empirical Methods on Natural Language Processing in Lisbon this weekend. It operates by separately generating a series of logical equations, which serve as components of possible answers, from the text and the diagram in the question. It then weighs the accuracy of the equations and tries to discern whether its interpretation of the diagram and text is strong enough to select one of the multiple-choice answers.

The Allen Institute approach has more in common with an earlier generation of artificial intelligence research that relied on logic and reasoning.

Moreover, the Allen Institute researchers said, machine-learning techniques have continued to fall short in areas where humans excel, such as problem solving.

"This is not pattern matching," said Oren Etzioni, a computer scientist and the chief executive of the Allen Institute.

While neural networks have made progress based on the availability of huge amounts of data online, the Allen Institute approach works with relatively sparse data (even all the standardized-test questions do not make up a big data set). The data is too sparse, in fact, to be broadly useful in solving school test questions in subjects that require reasoning — such as algebra and science disciplines — Mr. Etzioni said.

Ultimately, Dr. Marcus said, he believed that progress in artificial intelligence would require multiple tests, just as multiple tests are used to assess human performance.

"There is no one measure of human intelligence," he said. "Why should there be just one A.I. test?"

One open question is whether the incremental progress that is evident in the Allen Institute geometry-solving program is a significant step forward or whether it has more in common with a series of earlier proclamations in the field of "thinking machines" that ended in blind alleys.

In the 1960s, Hubert Dreyfus, a philosophy professor at the University of California, Berkeley, expressed this skepticism most clearly when he wrote, "Believing that writing these types of programs will bring us closer to real artificial intelligence is like believing that someone climbing a tree is making progress toward reaching the moon."

Artificial Intelligence Is Far From Matching Humans, Panel Says

BY JOHN MARKOFF | MAY 25, 2016

SEATTLE — Never mind Terminator-like killer robots. Artificial intelligence researchers are grappling with more realistic questions like whether their creations will take too many jobs from humans.

Eight years after leading artificial intelligence scientists said their field did not need to be regulated, the question of government oversight has re-emerged as the technology has rapidly progressed.

On Tuesday, at an event sponsored by the White House Office of Science and Technology Policy, legal specialists and technologists explored questions about autonomous systems that would increasingly make decisions without human input in areas like warfare, transportation and health.

Still, despite improvement in areas like machine vision and speech understanding, A.I. research is still far from matching the flexibility and learning capability of the human mind, researchers at the conference said.

"The A.I. community keeps climbing one mountain after another, and as it gets to the top of each mountain, it sees ahead still more mountains," said Ed Felten, a computer scientist who is a deputy chief technology officer in the Office of Science and Technology Policy.

The half-day program, co-sponsored with the University of Washington School of Law and the university's Tech Policy Lab, was the first of four events the White House has planned that will focus on law and policy, as well as the social and economic implications of autonomous machine research.

"These issues of A.I. and machines learning were popping up all over the government, and there was an opportunity to get more coordinated in how we address them," Dr. Felten said.

CHIP SOMODEVILLA/GETTY IMAGES

A semiautonomous robot created by students at Virginia Tech. At a conference on Tuesday sponsored by the White House Office of Science and Technology Policy, legal specialists and technologists said that research was still far from matching the flexibility and learning capability of the human mind.

After 25 artificial intelligence researchers met in 2009, the group, sponsored by the Association for the Advancement of Artificial Intelligence, reported that there was no imminent danger from a technology that had prompted fears of Hollywood-style weapons and advanced economies that were devoid of human workers.

Leading technologists and scientists have also pondered the possibility that artificial intelligence, like genetic engineering, might soon constitute an existential threat to the human race.

In recent years, the debate has spread to the broader social impact of autonomous programs that will perform tasks like driving cars and offering medical and financial advice.

One challenge for A.I., according to a number of the researchers who spoke, is that the public perception about the threat of A.I. has largely been shaped by Hollywood.

"Certainly, Hollywood has played a tremendous role with vision like Skynet," the computer network that turns on humans in the "Terminator" movies, said Oren Etzioni, chief executive of the Allen Institute for Artificial Intelligence, a nonprofit research group funded by the Microsoft co-founder Paul Allen. "It's pretty much always the case in science fiction that A.I. is this monolithic entity that is scheming to take over."

He cautioned that attention-getting feats like Google's AlphaGo program, which defeated a human champion in the board game Go, had plenty of humans behind the machine doing the work.

At the same time, despite the consensus about the limits of today's technology, many of the panelists wrestled with new challenges presented by A.I. systems that were appearing in virtually all walks of life, including services delivered by smartphones and algorithms that guide missiles.

Kate Crawford, a principal researcher at Microsoft Research, called on the industry to add ethics to the professional training of engineers. "We need to start changing the skill set of the people who are going to be the data scientists of the future and the A.I. creators of the future," she said.

"A.I. systems are pervasive," Ms. Crawford said, pointing to a doll like Hello Barbie, which speaks and listens.

"You might think that's a fantastic toy, that's really wonderful," she said. "What you don't realize is that it is the front to this huge data ingestion machine that is taking all of those statements by that child and then using them for a whole range of purposes."

The Robot Revolution Will Be the Quietest One

OPINION | BY LIU CIXIN | DEC. 7, 2016

Though the first fatal crash involving an autonomous car took place in July 2016, self-driving vehicles have been adopted around the world.

IN 2016, SELF-DRIVING CARS made inroads in several countries, many of which rewrote their laws to accommodate the new technology. As a science-fiction writer, it's my duty to warn the human race that the robot revolution has begun — even if no one has noticed yet.

When a few autonomous test cars appeared on the roads over the last few years, we didn't think of them as robots because they didn't have the humanoid shape that science-fiction movies taught us to expect. In 2016, they were adopted widely: as buses in the United Arab Emirates and the Netherlands, taxis in Singapore and private cars in the United States and China. There was a fatal accident in Florida involving an autonomous car, which caused some concerns, but this did not significantly affect our embrace of this technology.

Instead of arming ourselves against this alien presence, as some of my fellow science-fiction writers have fearfully suggested, we gawked as the vehicles pulled up to the curb. The driverless vehicles, some of which had no steering wheels or gas pedals, merged into traffic and stopped at stop signs, smoothly taking us to our destinations. We lounged in comfort, occasionally taking selfies.

Machine learning has been an important tool for autonomous car companies as they develop the systems that pilot their vehicles. Instead of rigidly following programming as an app on your phone does, an A.I. system can try to learn to do a task itself, using techniques borrowed from human learning, like pattern recognition and trial and error, and may use hardware modeled on the architecture of a human brain. Currently, the responsibilities of artificial intelligence are mostly limited to tasks like translating texts, helping with medical

RENAUD VIGOURT VIA THE NEW YORK TIMES

diagnoses and writing simple articles for media companies. But we can expect to see unimaginable progress in this field in future — and the widespread use of the autonomous car is going to accelerate that process as automobile and technology companies invest ever more resources in its development.

Let's try to envision that future. As during every other technological revolution, the robots will first transform our economy. People who drive for a living will lose their jobs — around 3 million in the United States alone. E-commerce may experience further booms because of automation, and car ownership is likely to become nearly obsolete as more targeted car sharing and public transportation systems are developed. Eventually, the robot cars could be integrated with other transportation systems. Say that you live in New York City and want to go to China's Henan Province: You will enter the address into an app, a car will take you to your plane at the airport, and after you land, another will take you directly to your destination.

Robots will begin to creep into other areas of our lives — serving as busboys or waiters, for example — as our investments in robotic transport improve their prowess in areas such as environmental detection and modeling, hyper-complex problem solving and fuzzy-logic applications. With every advance, the use of A.I.-powered robots will expand into other fields: health care, policing, national defense and education.

There will be scandals when things go wrong and backlash movements from the new Luddites. But I don't think we'll protest very much. The A.I. systems that drive our cars will teach us to trust machine intelligence over the human variety — car accidents will become very rare, for example — and when given an opportunity to delegate a job to a robot, we will placidly do so without giving it much thought.

In all previous technological revolutions, people who lost their jobs mostly moved to new ones, but that will be less likely when the robots take over. A.I. that can learn from experience will replace many accountants, lawyers, bankers, insurance adjusters, doctors, scientific researchers and some creative professionals. Intelligence and advanced training will no longer mean job stability.

Gradually the A.I. era will transform the essence of human culture. When we're no longer more intelligent than our machines, when they can easily outthink and outperform us, making the sort of intuitive leaps in research and other areas that we currently associate with genius, a sort of learned helplessness is likely to set in for us, and the idea of work itself may cease to hold meaning.

As A.I. takes over, the remaining jobs may dwindle to a fraction of what they were, employing perhaps 10 percent or even less of the total population. These may be highly creative or complex jobs that robots can't do, such as senior management, directing scientific research or nursing and child care.

In the dystopian scenario, as jobless numbers rise across the globe, our societies sink into prolonged turmoil. The world could be engulfed by endless conflicts between those who control the A.I. and the rest of us. The technocratic 10 percent could end up living in a gated community with armed robot guards.

There is a second, utopian scenario, where we've anticipated these changes and come up with solutions beforehand. Those in political power have planned a smoother, gentler transition, perhaps using A.I.

to help them anticipate and modulate the strife. At the end of it, almost all of us live on social welfare.

How we will spend our time is hard to predict. "He who does not work, neither shall he eat" has been the cornerstone of civilizations through the ages, but that will have vanished. History shows that those who haven't had to work — aristocrats, say — have often spent their time entertaining and developing their artistic and sporting talents while scrupulously observing elaborate rituals of dress and manners.

In this future, creativity is highly valued. We sport ever more fantastic makeup, hairstyles and clothing. The labor of past ages seems barbaric.

But the aristocrats ruled nations; in the A.I. era, machines are doing all the thinking. Because, over the decades, we've gradually given up our autonomy, step by step, allowing ourselves to be transformed into A.I.'s docile, fabulously pampered pets. As A.I. whisks us from place to place — visits to family members, art galleries and musical events — we will look out the windows, as unaware of its plans for us as a poodle on its way to the groomer's.

The science-fiction writer **LIU CIXIN** is a nine-time winner of the Galaxy Award, China's highest honor for science-fiction writing. He is the first Chinese writer to receive the Hugo Award for Best Novel, which he received for his international best seller "The Three-Body Problem." A 3-D film adaptation will be released in 2017.

These Are Not the Robots We Were Promised

OPINION | BY NICHOLAS CARR | SEPT. 9, 2017

FROM THE MOMENT we humans first imagined having mechanical servants at our beck and call, we've assumed they would be constructed in our own image. Outfitted with arms and legs, heads and torsos, they would perform everyday tasks that we'd otherwise have to do ourselves. Like the indefatigable maid Rosie on "The Jetsons," the officious droid C-3PO in "Star Wars" and the tortured "host" Dolores Abernathy in "Westworld," the robotic helpmates of popular culture have been humanoid in form and function.

It's time to rethink our assumptions. A robot invasion of our homes is underway, but the machines — so-called smart speakers like Amazon Echo, Google Home and the forthcoming Apple HomePod — look nothing like what we expected. Small, squat and stationary, they resemble vases or cat food tins more than they do people.

Echo and its ilk do, however, share a crucial trait with their imaginary forebears: They illuminate the times. Whatever their shape, robots tell us something important about our technologies and ourselves.

Although smart speakers have been around just three years, they already have a hold on us. The devices, powered by "chatbots" like Siri and Alexa, are in the midst of a sales boom. Some 35 million Americans now use the diminutive, talking computers — more than twice the number of just a year ago, according to estimates by eMarketer — and analysts predict that three-quarters of United States households will own at least one of the gadgets by 2020.

It's not hard to understand the attraction. Smart speakers are oracles of the countertop. They may not be able to speak for the gods, but they can deliver reports on news, traffic and weather. And they have other talents that their Delphic ancestor couldn't even dream of: They can serve as D.J. They can diagnose ailments and soothe anxieties. They can read bedtime stories.They can even bark like a watchdog to scare off burglars. And they promise to be the major-domos of home automation, adjusting lights, controlling appliances and issuing orders to specialized robots like the Roomba vacuum cleaner.

Still, if you were looking forward to having a Rosie scurrying around your abode, feather duster in hand, an Echo feels like a letdown. It just sits there.

There are good reasons that the domestic robot has taken such an uninspiring form. Some are technical. Visualizing a nimble, surefooted android is easy, but building one is hard. As the Carnegie Mellon professor Illah Nourbakhsh explains in his book "Robot Futures," it requires advances not only in artificial intelligence but also in the complex hardware systems required for movement, perception and dexterity.

The human nervous system is a marvel of physical control, able to sense and respond fluidly to an ever-changing environment. Achieving such agility with silicon and steel lies well beyond the reach of today's engineers. Even the most advanced of our current automatons still get flustered by mundane tasks like loading a dishwasher or dusting knickknacks.

Meanwhile, thanks to gains in networking, language processing and miniaturization, it has become simple to manufacture small, cheap computers that can understand basic questions and commands, gather and synthesize information from online databanks and control other electronics. The technology industry has enormous incentives to promote such gadgets. Now that many of the biggest tech companies operate like media businesses, trafficking in information, they're in a race to create new products to charm and track consumers.

Smart speakers provide a powerful complement to smartphones in this regard. Equipped with sensitive microphones, they serve as in-home listening devices — benign-seeming bugs — that greatly extend the companies' ability to monitor people's habits. Whenever you chat with a smart speaker, you're disclosing valuable information about your routines and proclivities.

Beyond the technical challenges, there's a daunting psychological barrier to constructing and selling anthropomorphic machines. No one has figured out how to bridge what computer scientists term the "uncanny valley" — the wide gap we sense between ourselves and imitations of ourselves. Because we're such social beings, our minds are exquisitely sensitive to the expressions, gestures and manners of others. Any whiff of artificiality triggers revulsion. Humanoid robots seem creepy to us, and the more closely they're designed to mimic us, the creepier they are. That puts roboticists in a bind: The more perfect their creations, the less likely we'll want them in our homes. Lacking human characteristics, smart speakers avoid the uncanny valley altogether.

Although they may not look like the robots we envisioned, smart speakers do have antecedents in our cultural fantasy life. The robot they most recall at the moment is HAL, the chattering eyeball in Stanley Kubrick's sci-fi classic "2001: A Space Odyssey." But their current form — that of a stand-alone gadget — is not likely to be their ultimate form. They seem fated to shed their physical housing and turn into a sort of ambient digital companion. Alexa will come to resemble Samantha, the "artificially intelligent operating system" that beguiles the Joaquin Phoenix character in the movie "Her." Through a network of speakers, microphones and sensors scattered around our homes, we'll be able to converse with our solicitous A.I. assistants wherever and whenever we like.

Mark Zuckerberg, the Facebook C.E.O., spent much of last year programming a prototype of such a virtual agent. In a video released in December, he gave a demo of the system. Walking around his Silicon Valley home, he conducted a running dialogue with his omnipresent chatbot, calling on it to supply him with a clean T-shirt and toast bread for his breakfast, play movies and music, and entertain his infant daughter. Hooked up to cameras with facial-recognition software, the digitized Jeeves also acted as a sentry for the Zuckerberg compound, screening visitors and unlocking the gate.

Whether real or fictional, robots hold a mirror up to society. If Rosie and her kin embodied a 20th-century yearning for domestic order and familial bliss, smart speakers symbolize our own, more self-absorbed time.

It seems apt that as we come to live more of our lives virtually, through social networks and other simulations, our robots should take the form of disembodied avatars dedicated to keeping us comfortable in our media cocoons. Even as they spy on us, the devices offer sanctuary from the unruliness of reality, with all its frictions and strains. They place us in a virtual world meticulously arranged to suit our bents and biases, a world that understands us and shapes itself to our desires. Amazon's decision to draw on classical mythology in naming its smart speaker was a masterstroke. Every Narcissus deserves an Echo.

NICHOLAS CARR is the author of "The Shallows" and "Utopia Is Creepy."

Google's A.I. Program Rattles Chinese Go Master as It Wins Match

BY PAUL MOZUR | MAY 25, 2017

HONG KONG — It's all over for humanity — at least in the game of Go.

For the second game in a row, a Google computer program called AlphaGo beat the world's best player of what many consider the world's most sophisticated board game. AlphaGo is scheduled to play its human opponent, the 19-year-old Chinese prodigy Ke Jie, one more time on Saturday in the best-of-three contest.

But with a score of 2-0 heading into that final game, and earlier victories against other opponents already on the books, AlphaGo has proved its superiority.

Discussing the contest afterward, Mr. Ke said a very human element got the better of him: his emotions. In the middle of the game, when he thought he might have had a chance at winning, he got too keyed up, he said.

"I was very excited. I could feel my heart bumping," Mr. Ke said after the contest, which took place in Wuzhen, near Shanghai. "Maybe because I was too excited I made some stupid moves."

"Maybe that's the weakest part of human beings," he added.

AlphaGo's victory on Thursday simply reinforced the progress and power of artificial intelligence to handle specific but highly complex tasks. Because of the sheer number of possible moves in Go, computer scientists thought until recently that it would be a decade before a machine could play better than a human master.

A small consolation for Mr. Ke was that he played a near-perfect game for the first hundred moves, according to the scientists who designed AlphaGo.

STR/STRINGER/AFP/GETTY IMAGES

The Chinese Go master Ke Jie during a game against AlphaGo, Google's artificial intelligence program, in Wuzhen, near Shanghai, in May 2017.

Still, like a sprinter who can at first keep pace with a train, in the end Mr. Ke was left in the dust by the computer.

Demis Hassabis, a co-founder of DeepMind — the artificial intelligence arm of Google's parent, Alphabet Incorporated, that created the software — said that as he watched how close the game was, his pulse rate went up as well.

AlphaGo of course has no heart and feels no nerves, and in the end that may have helped make the difference. Scientists and futurists have pointed to that cold focus as a major reason artificial intelligence may someday take over large numbers of white-collar jobs. Still, that detachment means AlphaGo lacks the human touch required to manage employees, counsel patients or adequately write flowing newspaper features about its own dominance over humans.

Tests of the technology in games like Go still mark an early step. Because the strategy options are limited to moves on a board, games like Go are particularly suited to the technology.

Computer scientists say that often the best use of artificial intelligence is not to pit it against humans, but to pair it with them.

To that end, two Go professionals, each teamed with AlphaGo, are scheduled to play against each other on Friday. Mr. Hassabis has said that top amateur Go players, with the help of AlphaGo, can generally manage to beat the software program in a match. In short, a human with a computer is still stronger than a computer.

Ke Jie has said that after the third game on Saturday, he will return to focusing on playing against humans, and is not likely to take on a computer again, arguing that the technology has become too formidable.

"After this time, AlphaGo to me is 100 percent perfection, to me AlphaGo is the god of the Go game," he said after the game on Thursday.

"For human beings," he added, "our understanding of this game is only very limited."

Busting the Myths About A.I. Invading Our Lives

BY CADE METZ | DEC. 13, 2017

HOW DO NEW YORK TIMES journalists use technology in their jobs and in their personal lives? Cade Metz, a technology reporter for The Times based in San Francisco, discussed the tech he is using.

Q: *You write a lot about artificial intelligence. What is the strongest A.I. product that people can use right now?*

A: A good thing to try is the digital assistant on the latest Google Pixel phone because it shows both the power of artificial intelligence and the limitations.

It is very good at recognizing what you say, and it responds in a voice that sounds more human than most computer noises we are used to. Researchers at a Google A.I. lab in London built a system that learns to speak by analyzing recordings of human voices and identifying the patterns that make them human.

But it still doesn't sound exactly like a human. And though the Google Assistant — like other digital assistants from the likes of Amazon and Apple — does a decent job of responding to some questions and commands, it is a long way from not just recognizing but actually understanding conversational speech.

That is the story of A.I. over the last five years. The improvements have been enormous. But there is still a very long way to go.

Q: *Do you use it at all to help you do your work?*

A: Nope. I reviewed the new Pixel phone. But I get along fine with my older Android phone. The irony is that I am a techno-skeptic.

At least in my own head, this makes good sense. I don't cover a consumer technology company. I cover the people and the ideas that

JIM WILSON/THE NEW YORK TIMES

Cade Metz, a technology reporter, at his desk in San Francisco. While enormous gains have been made in artificial intelligence, there is still a long way to go, he said.

are driving the next wave of technologies. And I took at where these technologies will take us — for better or for worse.

But here is what I would like: a service that automatically transcribes my recorded interviews. There are services that use humans to do this, but they're expensive. Speech recognition technology has improved to the point where machines should be able to quickly and accurately do this for me on the cheap.

Q: *What are the potential pitfalls of so much A.I. in our lives?*

A: They are myriad. The latest A.I. services, like the one that handles the voice for the Google Assistant, learn tasks by analyzing enormous amounts of data. By analyzing millions of llama photos, for instance, a system can learn to recognize a llama.

But this kind of machine learning can have unintended consequences. A few years back, Google got into trouble because its image recognition service identified some black people as gorillas.

What's more, researchers have shown that these kinds of systems can be fooled into seeing things that aren't there. That becomes an issue as the latest computer vision techniques find their way into security cameras, cars and other robotics.

The other worry is that the rise of certain technologies — including autonomous cars and other robotics — will significantly shift the job market. This is sure to happen at some point, but experts disagree on when.

Q: *Tech companies have hyped up virtual reality for the last few years. But VR is still mostly a gaming accessory. Do you think it will ever be used by everyday people?*

A: Like A.I., V.R. is overhyped. The difference is that A.I. is changing the everyday world in very real ways. Look at the Amazon Echo, the autonomous cars now being tested in places like the Phoenix area, the enormous improvements of widely used services like Google Translate. V.R. is, as you say, still mostly a gaming accessory.

There are some interesting possibilities, though. Therapists are using V.R. for exposure therapy, after two decades of published research in this area. Basically, it can help people conquer phobias or other conditions like post-traumatic stress disorder.

But everyday use? That is not happening anytime soon — especially for people like me, who wear glasses and don't like heavy equipment strapped to our heads.

Q: *What tech product do you love using in your daily life?*

A: Apple's iTunes. And the Amazon Kindle app. And Stitcher, a podcast app that reliably delivers everything from Revisionist History to archived episodes of Desert Island Discs. I also like my headphones.

The beauty of technology is that you can read, watch and listen to anything you want when you want it. Almost.

Q: *Some researchers are developing robots that learn on their own. Is Skynet inevitable?*

A: This fear is blown way out of proportion. But that might be a good thing. Though the Skynet scenario is unlikely to be a problem for many, many years — the far more immediate worry is the coming shift in the job markets from automation, and that is still years away — we certainly don't want Skynet catching us unawares.

That is why some researchers are already starting to think about what they call A.I. safety. They want to make sure that miscreants can't fool security cameras into seeing things that aren't there — and that A.I. systems can't prevent humans from flipping their off switch, however far away that possibility may be.

How Artificial Intelligence Is Edging Its Way Into Our Lives

BY THE NEW YORK TIMES | FEB. 12, 2018

IN PHOENIX, cars are self-navigating the streets. In many homes, people are barking commands at tiny machines, with the machines responding. On our smartphones, apps can now recognize faces in photos and translate from one language to another.

Artificial intelligence is here — and it's bringing new possibilities, while also raising questions. Do these gadgets and services really behave as advertised? How will they evolve in the years ahead? How quickly will they overhaul the way we live and change the way we do business?

The Times is exploring these matters this week at our annual New Work Summit, featuring technology executives, A.I. researchers, investors and others. Here are some of the key moments coming out of the conference, plus a rundown of some of our recent A.I. stories.

CADE METZ

HUAWEI STILL EAGER TO DO BUSINESS IN THE UNITED STATES

A month after the Chinese electronics giant Huawei suffered a big setback in its quest to sell its high-end smartphones to Americans, the company's chief for consumer devices, Richard Yu, said he was still optimistic about Huawei's prospects in the United States.

"We have won global consumers' trust, in over 170 countries," Mr. Yu said at the New Work Summit. "We very strictly protect consumers' privacy."

Huawei is the world's third-largest seller of smartphones and one of the planet's biggest suppliers of telecommunications equipment. But it has struggled for years to break into the United States.

A 2012 congressional report said that Huawei's network gear could be used by Beijing to spy on Americans, effectively cutting the company off from big buyers in the United States. In January, after lawmakers reiterated those concerns in a letter to the Federal Communications Commission, AT&T and Verizon walked away from deals to sell Huawei's latest phones.

At the conference on Tuesday, Mr. Yu said that Huawei had no ties to the Chinese government. "We are a globalized company, just headquartered in China," he said. "We are not part of any government. We have to be a company that is independent from every country."

Huawei would not be able to do business in so many places around the world without that independence, he said. "If we do something for one government, we will lose the trust of all governments."

RAYMOND ZHONG

HOW FACEBOOK IS USING A.I. TO FIGHT TROUBLEMAKERS

Mike Schroepfer, Facebook's chief technology officer, offered a glimpse of how the social network is applying artificial intelligence to ward off bad actors and keep its platform free of toxicity.

Calling the fight against rules violators a "cat and mouse game," Mr. Schroepfer said at the New Work Summit on Tuesday that Facebook's A.I. efforts had succeeded at certain types of content moderation, such as image classifier algorithms that find and automatically remove nude photos and videos.

Now on Facebook, he said, "the vast majority of nudity and pornography reporting is automatic."

But what about using A.I. to curb the spread of fake news? Facebook's director of artificial intelligence, Yann LeCun, said in 2016 that machine learning algorithms would one day be able to weed out false news on Facebook.

But the company has since added thousands of human content moderators and struck partnerships with human fact-checking organizations. Mr. Schroepfer implied Facebook has learned that A.I. alone would not do the trick, given the sophistication of bad actors who find ways around the platform's filters.

Mr. Schroepfer also said that human judgment would be required in certain situations, like a comment ("nice jacket") that could be either an earnest compliment or a sarcastic insult, depending on the context. And when it comes to some of Facebook's thornier problems, like trying to enforce consistent hate speech policies, human intervention may always be necessary.

"Whenever you are debating what your policy is, you're unlikely to build an A.I. that works well for that," he said.

KEVIN ROOSE

A CALL FOR REGULATORS TO STAND DOWN

Michael Kratsios, a deputy chief technology officer at the White House, said at the New Work Summit on Tuesday that regulators should get out of the way of advances in emerging technologies.

He cited progress toward a repeal of some regulations on commercial drones, such as rules prohibiting them from flying at night.

"For us, it's key to get ahead of those regulatory hurdles," said Mr. Kratsios, who previously worked as chief of staff to Peter Thiel, the libertarian venture capitalist. These regulations, he said, are "putting us at a disadvantage."

Unlike some experts who believe China is poised to dominate the A.I. age, Mr. Kratsios said he wasn't worried about overseas competition. The United States, he said, has a "30-year head start" in A.I. development.

And despite the White House's reputation for chaos and tumult, he maintained that it was "a great place to work."

KEVIN ROOSE

TECH GIANTS FACE A 'CRISIS OF TRUST'

Marc Benioff, the chief executive of Salesforce, blasted companies like Facebook on Tuesday for addicting children to their products and renewed his calls for more government regulation of the tech industry.

Mr. Benioff compared a new Facebook Messenger product for children to candy cigarettes, which he used to pretend to smoke as a boy.

"What do you think they were trying to get us to do with those?" Mr. Benioff asked onstage at the New Work Summit. "I don't think this is any different now. They're focused on the addictive nature of these user interfaces. At some point, we have to say, 'Hold on.' "

Silicon Valley is nearing the point where moral lines will have to be drawn by the government since the industry is not regulating itself and does not seem to be guided by a "strong hand of ethics," he said.

There is a "crisis of trust," he added, that will become a "tidal wave" among American consumers who are growing wary of tech giants.

"I'm trying to protect our industry," said Mr. Benioff, whose company sells access to business software over the internet. "If companies aren't able to regulate themselves, they should have external regulations."

One of the solutions he suggested was to move decision-making away from algorithms and back toward humans. He cited Facebook's decision to disband its trending news curation team as an example.

"Facebook had a team promoting, sorting and focusing stories, 100 curators that they removed and put an algorithm in their place, and that started the downward spiral that they're in today," Mr. Benioff said.

He also spoke about the recent ban on kegs of beer at Salesforce offices after he recently stumbled across one while visiting a company he had acquired.

"I view alcohol as a drug," he said. "The keg is not there anymore — well, actually who knows, but I hope it's not. I took a photo of the keg and put it on our social network and said, 'This is not who we are.' "

NELLIE BOWLES

SHOULD A.I. BE MORE 'HUMAN'?

Fei-Fei Li, a chief scientist at Google and a Stanford professor, has called on technologists to take a more "human centered" approach to the creation of artificial intelligence. On Tuesday at the New Work

Summit, Ms. Li said that researchers must work to ensure that A.I. embodied human qualities and that it would ultimately operate alongside humans, not replace them.

"I often tell my students not to be misled by the name 'artificial intelligence' — there is nothing artificial about it," she said. "A.I. is made by humans, intended to behave by humans and, ultimately, to impact humans lives and human society."

At Stanford, Ms. Li was instrumental in the recent rise of "computer vision" systems that can recognize people and objects entirely on their own. At Google, she is working to package and sell these and other systems as cloud computing services, delivering the latest A.I. technology to a wide range of businesses.

But she said that as Google and other internet giants pushed these techniques forward, academia and the government must help ensure that A.I. evolved into something that enhanced our humanity, created as many jobs as it replaced and operated in safe and predictable ways.

In particular, Ms. Li said, academic institutions can help ensure that computer scientists work alongside social scientists in building this new breed of technology.

"A.I. has outgrown its origin in computer science," she said.

Ultimately, said Ms. Li, who was born in China, A.I. reflects the people who build it more than other technologies do. For that reason and others, she said, A.I. researchers must work in a way that spans not only many industries but many cultures as well.

"I really believe there are no borders for science," she said.

CADE METZ

WHY AMERICAN TECH COMPANIES STRUGGLE IN CHINA

Tuesday's first speaker at the New Work Summit was Kai-Fu Lee, who used to lead Google in China and knows a thing or two about American tech giants in China. His prognosis about whether companies like Facebook will ever be able to crack the world's largest internet market?

"The American products are simply uncompetitive in the China market," said Mr. Lee, who is now chief executive of Sinovation Ventures, a venture capital firm focused on Chinese technology. Even if internet titans from the United States could operate in China, he said, the local competition means they would have a hard time thriving.

"Messenger is a much worse product than WeChat," he said, referring to Facebook's messaging app and Tencent's ubiquitous app for chatting, social networking, making payments and other tasks.

"Amazon in China is substantially worse than Taobao, JD and Tmall," he said, referring to three leading Chinese e-commerce sites. And, he said, "Apple Pay is much narrower and much harder to use than WeChat or Alipay."

Mr. Lee sees other issues that augur against a big Facebook or Google renaissance in China. Multinational companies tend not to hire local managers to lead their China operations. "They're not concerned about winning in the local market," he said.

GIULIA MARCHI FOR THE NEW YORK TIMES

A health care robot on display during the IFlyTek conference on A.I., held in Beijing in November.

Also, young Chinese these days would rather work for national champions like Alibaba or Tencent. Pitted against Chinese start-ups and big companies, where the hours tend to be long and the work culture cutthroat, the leading lights of American tech would get "get eaten for lunch."

RAYMOND ZHONG

TRUMP ADMINISTRATION SILENT ON A.I.

Last year, the Chinese government unveiled a plan to become the world leader in artificial intelligence by 2030, vowing to create a domestic industry worth $150 billion. This manifesto read like a challenge to the United States, and in many ways it echoed policies laid down by the Obama administration in 2016.

But as China pushes ahead in this area, many experts are concerned that the Trump administration is not doing enough to keep the United States ahead in the future. Although the big United States internet giants are leading the A.I. race, these experts believe the country as a whole could fall behind if does not do more to nurture research inside universities and government labs.

CADE METZ

WAYMO C.E.O. 'REALLY HAPPY' WITH UBER SETTLEMENT

John Krafcik, chief executive of the self-driving car company Waymo, took the stage at the New Work Summit on Monday night and spoke out for the first time since his company reached a settlement last week with Uber in a lawsuit over trade secrets that riveted Silicon Valley.

"We were really happy with the outcome that we engineered," Mr. Krafcik said. "We spent a lot of time in that case talking about the hardware, but the extra benefit we got from that suit was the ability to understand and ensure that Uber wasn't using any of our software."

He called the software Waymo's "secret sauce."

Waymo and Uber spent only four days at trial last week before settling, with Uber agreeing to provide Waymo 0.34 percent of its stock, worth about $245 million. The dispute between the companies started in 2016 when Uber bought Otto, a start-up founded by Anthony Levandowski, an early member of Google's self-driving car program. Waymo, which was spun out of Google, accused Mr. Levandowski of stealing technology before leaving and accused Uber of using the misappropriated knowledge.

"This was a really special case with a really special set of circumstances," Mr. Krafcik said. "For us, this was always about, and really just about, the fact that we needed to ensure Uber wasn't using our trade secrets." He added that he did not foresee Waymo suing other former employees.

Mr. Krafcik also discussed how Waymo was looking to start a ride-hailing service, which it is testing in Phoenix with thousands of driverless Pacifica minivans.

"We have a plan to move from city to city," he said. "We're not going to be launching with a 25 mile-per-hour product. We're talking about a full-speed service that will serve a very large geographic area with essentially unlimited pickup and drop-off points."

NELLIE BOWLES

NO, AMAZON ISN'T USING A.I. TO CUT JOBS

Jeff Wilke, Amazon's chief executive of its consumer business, which includes its e-commerce operations, doesn't often make public appearances. But on Monday night, he joined the New Work Summit to discuss the internet retailer's move into artificial intelligence.

His key message: A.I. is everywhere, but that doesn't mean it will take our jobs.

"If you look at the evolution of technology over the course of decades, tech doesn't eliminate work; it changes work," Mr. Wilke said.

He said that over the last five years, since Amazon bought

a robot maker called Kiva Systems, it had built 100,000 of the robots — and also hired 300,000 people. "We still need human judgment," he said.

Amazon has also embedded A.I. throughout the company, he added, with technologists working together with people who run businesses. The company is using machine learning and deep learnings, which are different flavors of A.I., to upgrade internal algorithms, he said.

As to how Amazon might use A.I. at Whole Foods, the grocery store chain that it said it would acquire last year, Mr. Wilke said little. When asked whether Amazon would integrate its cashier-less and A.I.-driven convenience store concept, called Amazon Go, with Whole Foods, he said, "I don't foresee the format of Whole Foods changing very much."

PUI-WING TAM

A.I. HAS BECOME A CAMPAIGN ISSUE

As A.I. technology barrels ahead in Silicon Valley, it's also starting to pick up steam as a political issue in Washington.

Over the weekend, I wrote about Andrew Yang, a former tech executive who has decided to run for president in 2020 as a Democrat on a "beware the robots" platform. He thinks that with innovations like self-driving cars and grocery stores without cashiers just around the corner, we're about to move into a frightening new era of mass unemployment and social unrest.

So he's proposing a universal basic income plan called the "Freedom Dividend," which would give every American adult $1,000 a month to guarantee them a minimum standard of living while they retrain themselves for new kinds of work.

Mr. Yang's campaign is a long shot, and there are significant hurdles to making universal basic income politically feasible. But the conversation about automation's social and economic consequences is long overdue. Even if he doesn't win the election, Mr. Yang may have hit on the next big political wedge issue.

KEVIN ROOSE

ARTIFICIAL INTELLIGENCE MAY BE BIASED

In modern artificial intelligence, data rules. A.I. software is only as smart as the data used to train it, as Steve Lohr recently wrote, and that means that some of the biases in the real world can seep into A.I.

If there are many more white men than black women in the system, for example, it will be worse at identifying the black women. That appears to be the case with some popular commercial facial recognition software.

Joy Buolamwini, a researcher at the M.I.T. Media Lab, found that the software can now tell if a white man in a photograph is male or female 99 percent of the time. But for darker skinned women, it is wrong nearly 35 percent of the time.

JOSEPH PLAMBECK

How to Make A.I. That's Good for People

OPINION | BY FEI-FEI LI | MARCH 7, 2018

FOR A FIELD that was not well known outside of academia a decade ago, artificial intelligence has grown dizzyingly fast. Tech companies from Silicon Valley to Beijing are betting everything on it, venture capitalists are pouring billions into research and development, and start-ups are being created on what seems like a daily basis. If our era is the next Industrial Revolution, as many claim, A.I. is surely one of its driving forces.

It is an especially exciting time for a researcher like me. When I was a graduate student in computer science in the early 2000s, computers were barely able to detect sharp edges in photographs, let alone recognize something as loosely defined as a human face. But thanks to the growth of big data, advances in algorithms like neural networks and an abundance of powerful computer hardware, something momentous has occurred: A.I. has gone from an academic niche to the leading differentiator in a wide range of industries, including manufacturing, health care, transportation and retail.

I worry, however, that enthusiasm for A.I. is preventing us from reckoning with its looming effects on society. Despite its name, there is nothing "artificial" about this technology — it is made by humans, intended to behave like humans and affects humans. So if we want it to play a positive role in tomorrow's world, it must be guided by human concerns.

I call this approach "human-centered A.I." It consists of three goals that can help responsibly guide the development of intelligent machines.

First, A.I. needs to reflect more of the depth that characterizes our own intelligence. Consider the richness of human visual perception. It's complex and deeply contextual, and naturally balances our awareness of the obvious with a sensitivity to nuance. By comparison, machine perception remains strikingly narrow.

Sometimes this difference is trivial. For instance, in my lab, an image-captioning algorithm once fairly summarized a photo as "a man riding a horse" but failed to note the fact that both were bronze sculptures. Other times, the difference is more profound, as when the same algorithm described an image of zebras grazing on a savanna beneath a rainbow. While the summary was technically correct, it was entirely devoid of aesthetic awareness, failing to detect any of the vibrancy or depth a human would naturally appreciate.

That may seem like a subjective or inconsequential critique, but it points to a major aspect of human perception beyond the grasp of our algorithms. How can we expect machines to anticipate our needs — much less contribute to our well-being — without insight into these "fuzzier" dimensions of our experience?

Making A.I. more sensitive to the full scope of human thought is no simple task. The solutions are likely to require insights derived from fields beyond computer science, which means programmers will have to learn to collaborate more often with experts in other domains.

Such collaboration would represent a return to the roots of our field, not a departure from it. Younger A.I. enthusiasts may be surprised to learn that the principles of today's deep-learning algorithms stretch back more than 60 years to the neuroscientific researchers David Hubel and Torsten Wiesel, who discovered how the hierarchy of neurons in a cat's visual cortex responds to stimuli.

Likewise, ImageNet, a data set of millions of training photographs that helped to advance computer vision, is based on a project called WordNet, created in 1995 by the cognitive scientist and linguist George Miller. WordNet was intended to organize the semantic concepts of English.

Reconnecting A.I. with fields like cognitive science, psychology and even sociology will give us a far richer foundation on which to base the development of machine intelligence. And we can expect the resulting technology to collaborate and communicate more naturally, which will help us approach the second goal of human-centered A.I.: enhancing us, not replacing us.

Imagine the role that A.I. might play during surgery. The goal need not be to automate the process entirely. Instead, a combination of smart software and specialized hardware could help surgeons focus on their strengths — traits like dexterity and adaptability — while keeping tabs on more mundane tasks and protecting against human error, fatigue and distraction.

Or consider senior care. Robots may never be the ideal custodians of the elderly, but intelligent sensors are already showing promise in helping human caretakers focus more on their relationships with those they provide care for by automatically monitoring drug dosages and going through safety checklists.

These are examples of a trend toward automating those elements of jobs that are repetitive, error-prone and even dangerous. What's left are the creative, intellectual and emotional roles for which humans are still best suited.

No amount of ingenuity, however, will fully eliminate the threat of job displacement. Addressing this concern is the third goal of human-centered A.I.: ensuring that the development of this technology is guided, at each step, by concern for its effect on humans.

Today's anxieties over labor are just the start. Additional pitfalls include bias against underrepresented communities in machine learning, the tension between A.I.'s appetite for data and the privacy rights of individuals and the geopolitical implications of a global intelligence race.

Adequately facing these challenges will require commitments from many of our largest institutions. Universities are uniquely positioned to foster connections between computer science and traditionally unrelated departments like the social sciences and even humanities, through interdisciplinary projects, courses and seminars. Governments can make a greater effort to encourage computer science education, especially among young girls, racial minorities and other groups whose perspectives have been underrepresented in A.I. And corporations should combine their aggressive investment in intelligent algorithms with ethical A.I. policies that temper ambition with responsibility.

No technology is more reflective of its creators than A.I. It has been said that there are no "machine" values at all, in fact; machine values are human values. A human-centered approach to A.I. means these machines don't have to be our competitors, but partners in securing our well-being. However autonomous our technology becomes, its impact on the world — for better or worse — will always be our responsibility.

FEI-FEI LI is a professor of computer science at Stanford, where she directs the Stanford Artificial Intelligence Lab, and the chief scientist for A.I. research at Google Cloud.

CHAPTER 2

A.I. Works

The point of A.I., according to many of its proponents, is to improve people's lives by taking over many of the mundane tasks of everyday life. Weak A.I. already does this, for example, whenever Siri answers a question or plays a song request or when Alexa places an order on Amazon. In the future, A.I. is likely to operate the vehicles that take people to work and transport goods. And strong A.I. may even take over more complex jobs in the medical and legal professions. What effects will A.I. have on jobs and economies? Will it in fact make life better for humans or simply leave them unemployed?

Will You Lose Your Job to a Robot? Silicon Valley Is Split

BY CLAIRE CAIN MILLER | AUG. 6, 2014

THERE IS LITTLE disagreement that machines are outworking humans. They have progressed from displacing factory workers to personal assistants and even lawyers, and much of our lives will be digitized or augmented even more in a decade.

The question for Silicon Valley is whether we're heading toward a robot-led coup or a leisure-filled utopia.

The Pew Research Center published a report Wednesday based on interviews with 2,551 people who make, research and analyze new technology. Most agreed that robotics and artificial intelligence would transform daily life by 2025, but respondents were almost evenly split about what that might mean for the economy and employment.

On one side were the techno-optimists. They believe that even though machines will displace many jobs in a decade, technology and human ingenuity will produce many more, as happened after the agricultural and industrial revolutions. The meaning of "job" might change, too, if people find themselves with hours of free time because the mundane tasks that fill our days are automated.

The other half agree that some jobs will disappear, but they are not convinced that new ones will take their place, even for some highly skilled workers. They fear a future of widespread unemployment, deep inequality and violent uprisings — particularly if policy makers and educational institutions don't step in.

Following are a sampling of the points of view expressed in the Pew report.

MOST UTOPIAN:

"How unhappy are you that your dishwasher has replaced washing dishes by hand, your washing machine has displaced washing clothes by hand or your vacuum cleaner has replaced hand cleaning? My guess is this 'job displacement' has been very welcome, as will the 'job displacement' that will occur over the next 10 years. This is a good thing. Everyone wants more jobs and less work."

HAL VARIAN, chief economist at Google

MOST DYSTOPIAN:

"We're going to have to come to grips with a long-term employment crisis and the fact that — strictly from an economic point of view, not a moral point of view — there are more and more 'surplus humans.' "

KARL FOGEL, partner at Open Tech Strategies, an open-source technology firm

MOST HOPEFUL:

"Advances in A.I. [artificial intelligence] and robotics allow people to cognitively offload repetitive tasks and invest their attention and energy in things where humans can make a difference. We already have cars that talk to us, a phone we can talk to, robots that lift the elderly out of bed and apps that remind us to call Mom. An app can dial Mom's number and even send flowers, but an app can't do that most human of all things: emotionally connect with her."

PAMELA RUTLEDGE, director of the Media Psychology Research Center, a nonprofit

MOST GRIM:

"The degree of integration of A.I. into daily life will depend very much, as it does now, on wealth. The people whose personal digital devices are day-trading for them, and doing the grocery shopping and sending greeting cards on their behalf, are people who are living a different life than those who are worried about missing a day at one of their three jobs due to being sick, and losing the job and being unable to feed their children."

Google self-driving vehicles won't have a steering wheel, accelerator pedal or brake pedal because they won't need them. Perhaps taxi drivers won't be needed as well.

BILL WOODCOCK, executive director for the Packet Clearing House, a nonprofit research institute on Internet traffic

MOST FRIGHTENING TO AMERICANS:

"Globally, more jobs will be created by manufacturing of robots, but in developed countries like the U.S. and Europe jobs will be displaced by manufacturing by robots."

MIKE LIEBHOLD, distinguished fellow at the Institute for the Future, a nonprofit research group

MOST FRIGHTENING TO PARENTS:

"Only the best-educated humans will compete with machines. And education systems in the U.S. and much of the rest of the world are still sitting students in rows and columns, teaching them to keep quiet and memorize what is told to them, preparing them for life in a 20th century factory."

HOWARD RHEINGOLD, tech writer and analyst

MOST FRIGHTENING TO COLLEGE STUDENTS:

"We hardly dwell on the fact that someone trying to pick a career path that is not likely to be automated will have a very hard time making that choice. X-ray technician? Outsourced already, and automation in progress. The race between automation and human work is won by automation."

JERRY MICHALSKI, founder of the Relationship Economy eXpedition

MOST FRIGHTENING TO HUMANS:

"Robotic sex partners will be commonplace. ... The central question of 2025 will be: What are people for in a world that does not need their labor, and where only a minority are needed to guide the 'bot-based economy?'"

STOWE BOYD, lead researcher for GigaOM Research

MOST COMPLIMENTARY TOWARD HUMANS:

"Employment will be mostly very skilled labor — and even those jobs will be continuously whittled away by increasingly sophisticated machines. Live, human salespeople, nurses, doctors, actors will be symbols of luxury, the silk of human interaction as opposed to the polyester of simulated human contact."

JUDITH DONATH, fellow at Harvard University's Berkman Center for Internet & Society

MOST FRIGHTENING TO MEN:

"The biggest exception will be jobs that depend upon empathy as a core capacity — schoolteacher, personal service worker, nurse. These jobs are often those traditionally performed by women. One of the bigger social questions of the mid-late 2020s will be the role of men in this world."

JAMAIS CASCIO, technology writer and futurist

MOST SKEPTICAL:

"As an engineering community, we've been working on robotics and A.I. for a long time. The rationale behind today's optimism is that with every technology generation, Moore's Law brings us closer to having enough computational resources to solve these problems well. But 2025 feels too soon — it takes decades for fundamental ideas like quantum mechanics to be fully worked out by a research community."

JOHN LAZZARO, visiting lecturer in computer science at the University of California, Berkeley

MOST REASSURING:

"The technodeterminist-negative view, that automation means jobs loss, end of story, versus the technodeterminist-positive view, that more and better jobs will result, both seem to me to make the error of confusing potential outcomes with inevitability. A technological advance by itself can either be positive or negative for jobs, depending on the social structure as a whole. This is not a technological consequence; rather, it's a political choice."

SETH FINKELSTEIN, software programmer and consultant

Can a Computer Replace Your Doctor?

BY ELISABETH ROSENTHAL | SEPT. 20, 2014

AS A FORMER PHYSICIAN, I shivered a bit when I heard Dr. Vivek Wadhwa say he would rather have an artificial-intelligence doctor than a human one. "I would trust an A.I. over a doctor any day," he proclaimed at a recent health innovation conference in San Francisco, noting that artificial intelligence provided "perfect knowledge." When asked to vote, probably a third of those in attendance agreed.

But it made sense: Dr. Wadhwa is a professor, entrepreneur and technology visionary. What's more, the conference took place in San Francisco, where faith in the power of technology and data to solve problems holds unshakable sway.

There was certainly plenty of innovation on display at the conference's rooftop reception, called "Health by the Numbers": One device attaches to your iPhone and turns it into an otoscope so you can see if your child has an ear infection; another allows it to check your blood alcohol level. Attendees could check out home cholesterol test kits, and a wearable device to track the "quality" of their breathing.

Silicon Valley is bringing a host of new data-driven technologies to health care, many of them with enormous potential. But before we rush to measure every human attribute in real time, it would be a good idea to ask: When is more data actually useful to promote and ensure better health? And when does technology add true value to health care? The results have been mixed.

"It holds great promise and excitement, but so far everyone is often disappointed with the outcomes," said Steven J. Van Kuiken, a director at McKinsey and Company who studies technology and health care. "There are lots of interesting ideas, but how do you get data that's useful to patients, physicians or regulators? And then how do you get them to act on it?"

While the proliferation of fitness trackers suggests there is commercial potential in consumer health data technology, utility may be limited. "I don't doubt the wearable piece is going to be a productive business model for people," Ian T. Clark, chief executive of Genentech, said at the conference. "I just don't know whether it's going to bend the curve in health outcomes."

Last month Aetna announced it was discontinuing CarePass, its personalized health data platform for patients, because it hadn't delivered on anticipated results. And some studies show that half the people who buy portable fitness trackers stop using them in a matter of months. That is probably because most people who wear them are already health-conscious and there may be little long-term value once they take note of their activity patterns, Mr. Van Kuiken suggested.

So how can we create innovative new technologies that will revolutionize health rather than end up as discarded Christmas presents?

One big challenge is that the elusive state we call "health" is not always easily measurable. Normal blood pressure jumps up and down in response to thoughts, hydration and stress. Some healthy people have low platelets or slight elevations of liver enzymes.

In some cases, the ability to collect data has outpaced medical understanding. There is no "normal" testosterone level for an aging male, yet millions of men have been told they suffer from a condition called Low T and are using testosterone gels, even though medical studies have shown the products are dangerous.

In other cases, the data can show up fine, even when the patient is not. You don't always measure the right thing. When I was in medical school, there was a gallows joke that some patients die with "Harvard numbers." In other words, the lab tests that were ordered were all perfect, but the patient died anyway.

On the other hand, the test results can look bad even when the patient is fine. Scans of the spine, for example, show that many people have big bulging discs but no back pain. So which do you treat, the M.R.I. or the patient?

One central rule of doctoring is that you only gather data that will affect your treatment. There are now devices that track the activity of your sympathetic nervous system as a measure of stress. But what do you do with that information? Other devices continuously monitor breathing for wheezing that isn't noticed or audible. Does that matter? Some studies have shown that continuous monitoring isn't useful for children hospitalized with bronchial infections.

If you were dieting, would stepping on the scale 1,000 times a day help you lose weight? Or consider the treatment of an abnormal heart rhythm. It's true that constant monitoring for a few days can be highly useful to identify the pattern and what provokes the attacks. After that, though, for many patients a wearable cardiac tracker might simply record normal beats that normal people experience all the time, increasing anxiety for many patients.

Everyone agrees, of course, that useful technology can be lifesaving.

At the Mayo Clinic's Transform symposium this month in Rochester, Minn., I heard Eric Dishman, a general manager at Intel, explain how he had used data to individualize his own cancer care. More than a decade ago, when he was only partly responding to chemotherapy for a rare kidney cancer, he used a step monitor to help figure out what provoked his pain and then worked with a physical therapist to treat it. More recently, scientists were able to analyze the genetic sequence of his tumor, identifying a medicine for treatment. He is now cancer free.

Likewise, continuous glucose monitors alert sleeping diabetics when their blood sugar drops too low. And some companies are developing chips and other technologies that can perform tests on a drop of blood — perfect for use in remote areas where sterile needles and full laboratories are not available.

There are also apps that provide data for researchers, including one that tracks the movement of asthma patients to see what provokes attacks. That could also help doctors better understand patterns of disease and allow them to adjust doses of medicine, Mr. Van Kuiken said.

So hurrah for technology. But it's just a tool. Let's hope we have the wisdom to ignore it, as we would a GPS device, when it leads us in the wrong direction — or nowhere at all.

The End of Lawyers? Not So Fast.

BY JOHN MARKOFF | JAN. 4, 2016

LAWYERS HAVE BEEN described as the canaries in the coal mine in the face of a wave of automation now beginning to displace highly skilled white-collar workers.

In recent years, the increasing reliance on so-called "e-discovery" software in lawsuits raised the specter that $35-an-hour paralegals as well as $400-an-hour lawyers would fall victim to programs that could read and analyze legal documents more quickly and accurately than humans.

The fate of lawyers has been seen as a harbinger of a broader wave of worker displacement. The rapid commercialization of a new generation of artificial intelligence-derived technologies has led to concerns that technological disruption will extend from white- and blue-collar occupations of largely routine work that can be automated, into highly-paid professions like legal workers and doctors.

That has led to a new round of automation anxiety. Two Massachusetts Institute of Technology economists, Eric Brynjolfsson and Andrew McAfee, and a Silicon Valley software entrepreneur, Martin Ford, have written several books among them — including "Race Against the Machine," "The Second Machine Age," "The Lights in the Tunnel" and "Rise of the Robots," warning that rapid technological advances might wreak havoc with the economy.

Not so fast.

Despite the fears of some of a "jobs-pocalypse," the economy has stubbornly refused to cooperate with the doomsayers. Last month, there were 149 million people employed in the United States, the most in history. And in recent months a growing array of new studies have indicated that the relationship between technological advances and job displacement is more complex and nuanced than pessimists have suggested.

In November, for example, a study prepared by McKinsey & Company suggested that adding technology to the workplace is more likely to transform, rather than eliminate, jobs. This echoed a growing consensus that it is important to distinguish "task" automation from "job" automation.

The McKinsey study found that less than 5 percent of jobs can be completely automated based on existing technologies within the next three to five years. Even more striking is a similar study by James Bessen, a Boston University School of Law researcher, who found a positive relationship between the degree of computerization in a particular job category and employment growth.

Those studies support another recent paper written by David Autor, an M.I.T. labor economist known for his research indicating that middle-income, mid-skilled jobs in the United States have undergone a significant decline in recent years.

But writing in the Journal of Economic Perspectives this summer, Mr. Autor posed the question: "Why are there still so many jobs?" He pointed out that automation just as frequently complements as replaces labor in the workplace. He predicted that in the future, while A.I. technologies would continue to replace routinized jobs, they would also increase the number of workers whose jobs require problem-solving, flexibility and creativity.

Earlier, Dr. Autor had written about what he described as the limits of automation technologies. The challenge for A.I. designers, he wrote, was embedded in the observation made by the pre-modern-computing era philosopher Michael Polanyi: "We can know more than we can tell …" In other words, there are many human activities that cannot be formally described. It is those aspects of human behavior that computers cannot be programmed to simulate.

That view is supported by a new study, "Can Robots Be Lawyers?", a draft of which was posted last week on the Social Science Research Network by Dana Remus, a professor at the University of North Carolina School of Law, and Frank S. Levy, an M.I.T. labor economist. In the study, they explored which aspects of a lawyer's job could be automated. The research suggested that, for now, even the most advanced A.I. technology would at best make only modest inroads into the legal profession. Based on their analysis of actual billed hours, the researchers examined the work that lawyers do in broad general categories. They then analyzed how much of each category might be displaced by existing A.I. and automation technologies.

As it turns out, being a lawyer involves performing a range of tasks, from reading and analyzing documents, to counseling, appearing in court and persuading juries. Indeed, reading documents accounts for a relatively modest portion of a lawyer's activities.

The researchers noted that many of the tasks that lawyers perform fall well within what Polanyi defined as human behavior that cannot be easily codified. "When a task is less structured, as many tasks are," the researchers wrote, "it will often be impossible to anticipate all possible contingencies."

And current e-discovery software programs still require significant involvement on the part of human lawyers, they wrote.

In an analysis of actual legal work practices from billing invoice data, the researchers estimated that about 13 percent of all legal work might ultimately fall prey to automation. If that amount of work disappeared in a single year, it would be devastating, of course. But implemented over many years, this amount of technological change would be less noticeable, they said.

They added that even in the case of start-ups like LegalZoom and Rocket Lawyer, two sites that can aid in the preparation of legal documents, the impact of automation would more likely be in expanding into underserved markets rather than in displacing existing legal services.

Artificial intelligence technologies will continue to wend their way into the workplace, but they are more likely to change work, rather than end it. "Even where automation has made significant progress, its impact has been far less than the headlines would have us believe," the authors of "Can Robots Be Lawyers?" wrote.

A.I. Is Doing Legal Work. But It Won't Replace Lawyers, Yet.

BY STEVE LOHR | MARCH 19, 2017

IMPRESSIVE ADVANCES in artificial intelligence technology tailored for legal work have led some lawyers to worry that their profession may be Silicon Valley's next victim.

But recent research and even the people working on the software meant to automate legal work say the adoption of A.I. in law firms will be a slow, task-by-task process. In other words, like it or not, a robot is not about to replace your lawyer. At least, not anytime soon.

"There is this popular view that if you can automate one piece of the work, the rest of the job is toast," said Frank Levy, a labor economist at the Massachusetts Institute of Technology. "That's just not true, or only rarely the case."

An artificial intelligence technique called natural language processing has proved useful in scanning and predicting what documents will be relevant to a case, for example. Yet other lawyers' tasks, like advising clients, writing legal briefs, negotiating and appearing in court, seem beyond the reach of computerization, for a while.

"Where the technology is going to be in three to five years is the really interesting question," said Ben Allgrove, a partner at Baker McKenzie, a firm with 4,600 lawyers. "And the honest answer is we don't know."

Dana Remus, a professor at the University of North Carolina School of Law, and Mr. Levy studied the automation threat to the work of lawyers at large law firms. Their paper concluded that putting all new legal technology in place immediately would result in an estimated 13 percent decline in lawyers' hours.

A more realistic adoption rate would cut hours worked by lawyers by 2.5 percent annually over five years, the paper said. The research also suggests that basic document review has already been outsourced or automated at large law firms, with only 4 percent of lawyers' time now spent on that task.

Their gradualist conclusion is echoed in broader research on jobs and technology. In January, the McKinsey Global Institute found that while nearly half of all tasks could be automated with current technology, only 5 percent of jobs could be entirely automated. Applying its definition of current technology — widely available or at least being tested in a lab — McKinsey estimates that 23 percent of a lawyer's job can be automated.

Technology will unbundle aspects of legal work over the next decade or two rather than the next year or two, legal experts say. Highly paid lawyers will spend their time on work on the upper rungs of the legal task ladder. Other legal services will be performed by nonlawyers — the legal equivalent of nurse practitioners — or by technology.

Corporate clients often are no longer willing to pay high hourly rates to law firms for junior lawyers to do routine work. Those tasks are already being automated and outsourced, both by the firms themselves and by outside suppliers like Axiom, Thomson Reuters, Elevate and the Big Four accounting firms.

So the law firm partner of the future will be the leader of a team, "and more than one of the players will be a machine," said Michael Mills, a lawyer and chief strategy officer of a legal technology start-up called Neota Logic.

SURPRISING SPREAD

The pace of technology improvement is notoriously unpredictable. For years, labor economists said routine work like a factory job could be reduced to a set of rules that could be computerized. They assumed that professionals, like lawyers, were safe because their work was wrapped in language.

But advances in artificial intelligence overturned that assumption. Technology unlocked the routine task of sifting through documents, looking for relevant passages.

So major law firms, sensing the long-term risk, are undertaking initiatives to understand the emerging technology and adapt and exploit it.

Dentons, a global law firm with more than 7,000 lawyers, established an innovation and venture arm, Nextlaw Labs, in 2015. Besides monitoring the latest technology, the unit has invested in seven legal technology start-ups.

"Our industry is being disrupted, and we should do some of that ourselves, not just be a victim of it," John Fernandez, chief innovation officer of Dentons, said.

Last month, Baker McKenzie set up an innovation committee of senior partners to track emerging legal technology and set strategy. Artificial intelligence has stirred great interest, but law firms today are using it mainly in "search-and-find type tasks" in electronic discovery, due diligence and contract review, Mr. Allgrove said.

More than 280 legal technology start-ups have raised $757 million since 2012, according to the research firm CB Insights.

At many of these start-ups, the progress is encouraging but measured, and each has typically focused on a specific area of law, like bankruptcy or patents, or on a certain legal task, like contract review. Their software learns over time, but only after it has been painstakingly trained by human experts.

When Alexander Hudek, a computer scientist whose résumé includes heavyweight research like working on the human genome project, turned to automating the review of legal contracts in 2011, he figured that he would tweak standard algorithms and that it would be a four-month job.

Instead, it took two and a half years to refine the software so it could readily identify concepts such as noncompete contract clauses and change-of-control, said Mr. Hudek, chief technology officer of Kira Systems.

The Kira program sharply winnows the number of documents read by people, but human scrutiny is still required.

Yet the efficiency gains can be striking. Kira's clients report reducing the lawyer time required for contract review by 20 percent to 60 percent, said Noah Waisberg, chief executive of Kira.

In Miami, Luis Salazar, a partner in a five-lawyer firm, began using software from the start-up Ross Intelligence in November in his bankruptcy practice. Ask for the case most similar to the one you have and the Ross program, which taps some of IBM's Watson artificial intelligence technology, reads through thousands of cases and delivers a ranked list of the most relevant ones, Mr. Salazar said.

Skeptical at first, he tested Ross against himself. After 10 hours of searching online legal databases, he found a case whose facts nearly mirrored the one he was working on. Ross found that case almost instantly.

Mr. Salazar has been particularly impressed by a legal memo service that Ross is developing. Type in a legal question and Ross replies a day later with a few paragraphs summarizing the answer and a two-page explanatory memo.

The results, he said, are indistinguishable from a memo written by a lawyer. "That blew me away," Mr. Salazar said. "It's kind of scary. If it gets better, a lot of people could lose their jobs."

Not yet. The system is pretty good at identifying the gist of questions and cases, but Ross is not much of a writer, said Jimoh Ovbiagele, the chief technology officer of Ross. Humans take the rough draft that Ross produces and create the final memos, which is why it takes a day.

The start-up's engineers are trying to fully automate the memo-writing process, but Mr. Ovbiagele said, "We are a long way from there at this point."

THE GOOD OLD DAYS

James Yoon, a lawyer in Palo Alto, Calif., recalls 1999 as the peak of the old way of lawyering. A big patent case then, he said, might have needed the labor of three partners, five associates and four paralegals.

Today, a comparable case would take one partner, two associates and one paralegal.

Two obvious factors have led to that downsizing: tightened legal spending and digital technologies that automated some tasks, like document searches, said Mr. Yoon, a partner at Wilson Sonsini Goodrich & Rosati.

Mr. Yoon uses software tools like Lex Machina and Ravel Law to guide litigation strategy in his patent cases. These programs pore through court decisions and filing data to make profiles and predictions about judges and lawyers.

What are the chances a certain motion will be approved by a particular judge, based on all his or her past rulings? Does the opposing counsel go to trial often or usually settle cases?

Mr. Yoon compares what he does to the way baseball and football analysts assess the tendencies of players and coaches on other teams.

The clever software, he said, is "changing how decisions are made, and it's changing the profession."

But its impact on employment would seem to be far less than, say, electronic discovery. The data-driven analysis technology is assisting human work rather than replacing it. Indeed, the work that consumes most of Mr. Yoon's time involves strategy, creativity, judgment and empathy — and those efforts cannot yet be automated.

Mr. Yoon, who is 49, stands as proof. In 1999, his billing rate was $400 an hour. Today, he bills at $1,100 an hour.

"For the time being, experience like mine is something people are willing to pay for," Mr. Yoon said. "What clients don't want to pay for is any routine work."

But, he added, "the trouble is that technology makes more and more work routine."

Of Lawyers and Robots

LETTER | BY DOV GREENBAUM | APRIL 3, 2017

TO THE EDITOR:

Re "A.I. Is Doing Legal Work. But It Won't Replace Lawyers, Yet." (Business Day, March 20):

It shouldn't come as a surprise that the unrelenting march of technology — specifically, artificial intelligence, or A.I. — would eventually affect the legal market and other white-collar professions.

But what is different now from, say, the introduction of automobiles at the expense of horse-driven cabs is the sheer magnitude of all those affected by A.I.

Consider the millions of transportation-related jobs that will be disrupted by the rapidly approaching introduction of self-driving cars and trucks. There aren't too many options.

While some have proposed a stopgap method of taxing employers who replace human workers with robots, better solutions include providing training and re-education for those who can move on to other jobs, and a universal basic income for those who can't.

For the lawyers in particular, incoming law students must demand that their education provide them with the tools to adapt before they end up with hundreds of thousands of dollars in student debt and a disappearing profession.

DOV GREENBAUM
Herzliya, Israel

The writer is director of the Zvi Meitar Institute for Legal Implications of Emerging Technologies.

A Robot for a Lawyer?

LETTER | BY PAUL E. KERSON | APRIL 7, 2017

TO THE EDITOR:

I read "Of Lawyers and Robots" (letter, nytimes.com, April 3) with great interest (and a chuckle).

Shall we have a robot show up at the night arraignment when Junior is locked up for crashing his car and injuring others while texting? Shall the robot counsel Junior in his jail cell and plead with the judge for bail?

Want a robot holding your hand through a bitter divorce proceeding? How about a robot when the siblings are in a vicious dispute over Mom's estate?

And when the business partners are fighting over money (what else?), jeopardizing the jobs of their hundred employees, shall we send in one robot or two?

Paralegals sorting documents into piles is another matter. Computers can help sort. But reading potential documentary evidence and assessing its significance is a lawyer's personal responsibility and cannot be delegated to a machine (unless the client wants to lose the case).

Lawyers hold this society together when serious problems between and among people arise. This is the last profession where artificial intelligence belongs, unless of course, we want artificial justice. We call that dictatorship, and we raise armies against it.

PAUL E. KERSON
Forest Hills, Queens

The writer has been a lawyer for 41 years so far.

Meet the People Who Train the Robots (to Do Their Own Jobs)

BY DAISUKE WAKABAYASHI | APRIL 28, 2017

SAN FRANCISCO — What if part of your job became teaching a computer everything you know about doing someone's job — perhaps your own?

Before the machines become smart enough to replace humans, as some people fear, the machines need teachers. Now, some companies are taking the first steps, deploying artificial intelligence in the workplace and asking their employees to train the A.I. to be more human.

We spoke with five people — a travel agent, a robotics expert, an engineer, a customer-service representative and a scriptwriter, of sorts — who have been put in this remarkable position. More than most, they understand the strengths (and weaknesses) of artificial intelligence and how the technology is changing the nature of work.

Here are their stories.

'IT MADE ME FEEL COMPETITIVE'

Rachel Neasham, travel agent

Ms. Neasham, one of 20 (human) agents at the Boston-based travel booking app Lola, knew that the company's artificial intelligence computer system — its name is Harrison — would eventually take over parts of her job. Still, there was soul-searching when it was decided that Harrison would actually start recommending and booking hotels.

At an employee meeting late last year, the agents debated what it meant to be human, and what a human travel agent could do that a machine couldn't. While Harrison could comb through dozens of hotel options in a blink, it couldn't match the expertise of, for example, a human agent with years of experience booking family vacations to Disney World. The human can be more nimble — knowing, for instance,

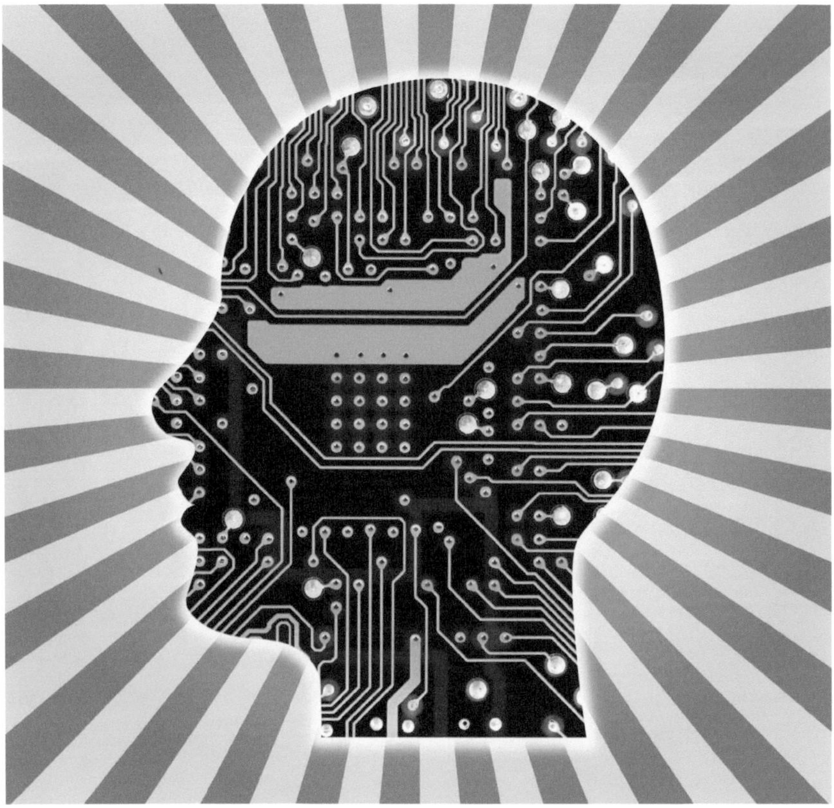

MINH UONG/THE NEW YORK TIMES

to advise a family that hopes to score an unobstructed photo with the children in front of the Cinderella Castle that they should book a breakfast reservation inside the park, before the gates open.

Ms. Neasham, 30, saw it as a race: Can human agents find new ways to be valuable as quickly as the A.I. improves at handling parts of their job? "It made me feel competitive, that I need to keep up and stay ahead of the A.I.," Ms. Neasham said. On the other hand, she said, using Harrison to do some things "frees me up to do something creative."

Ms. Neasham is no ordinary travel agent. When she left the Army after serving as a captain in Iraq and Afghanistan, she wanted to work at a start-up. She joined Lola as one of its first travel agents. Knowing that part of her job was to be a role model, basically, for Harrison, she felt a responsibility for Harrison to become a useful tool.

Founded in 2015 by Paul English, who also started the travel-search site Kayak, Lola was conceived as part automated chat service and part recommendation engine. Underlying it all was a type of artificial intelligence technology called machine learning.

Lola was set up so that agents like Ms. Neasham didn't interact with the A.I. much, but it was watching and learning from every customer interaction. Over time, Lola discovered that Harrison wasn't quite ready to take over communication with customers, but it had a knack for making lightning-fast hotel recommendations.

At first, Harrison would recommend hotels based on obvious customer preferences, like brands associated with loyalty programs. But then it started to find preferences that even the customers didn't realize they had. Some people, for example, preferred a hotel on the corner of a street versus midblock.

And in a coming software change, Lola will ask lifestyle questions like "Do you use Snapchat?" to glean clues about hotel preferences. Snapchat users tend to be younger and may prefer modern but inexpensive hotels over more established brands like the Ritz-Carlton.

While Harrison may make the reservations, the human agents support customers during the trip. Once the room is booked, the humans, for example, can call the hotel to try to get room upgrades or recommend how to get the most out of a vacation.

"That's something A.I. can't do," Ms. Neasham said.

'HOW DO WE ELEGANTLY RECOVER?'

Diane Kim, interaction designer

Ms. Kim is adamant: Her assistant doesn't use slang or emoji.

Her assistant, Andrew Ingram, also avoids small talk and doesn't waste time on topics beside scheduling her meetings, she said.

Ms. Kim isn't being tyrannical. She just knows her assistant better than most bosses, because she programmed him.

Ms. Kim, 22, works as an A.I. interaction designer at x.ai, a New York-based start-up offering an artificial intelligence assistant to help people schedule meetings. X.ai pitches clients on the idea that, through A.I., they get the benefits of a human assistant — saving the time and hassle of scheduling a meeting — at a fraction of the price.

It's Ms. Kim's job to craft responses for the company's assistants, who are named Andrew and Amy Ingram, or A.I. for short, that feel natural enough that swapping emails with these computer systems feels no different than emailing with a human assistant.

Ms. Kim's job — part playwright, part programmer and part linguist — didn't exist before Alexa, Siri and other A.I. assistants. The job is like a translator of sorts. It is to help humans access the A.I.'s superhuman capabilities like 24/7 availability and infallible memory without getting tripped up by robotic or awkward language.

Even in the narrow parameters of scheduling meetings, it takes a lot of machine learning to break down emails for a computer. For example, setting a meeting for "Wednesday" is different than setting a meeting for "a Wednesday," as in any Wednesday. X.ai breaks down emails to their component parts to understand intent.

The automated response is where Ms. Kim takes over. Her job is to imagine how a human assistant would arrange a meeting for the boss. For a specific task, she devises different situations — for example, what if the meeting had five attendees versus two — and then she creates a flow chart of how the email exchange would go.

The goal is to schedule a meeting in as few emails as possible. With that in mind, x.ai settled on a set of personality traits for its assistants: polite, professional, friendly and clear.

Sometimes, it's hard to predict what will rub people the wrong way. Early on, the A.I. assistant sent emails to potential attendees saying that the assistant would be happy to put something on the boss's "calendar," but some people found that wording to be cold, and not always appropriately deferential to the other attendees.

X.ai changed the wording so that the A.I. assistant says it would be happy to "find a time" that works for all attendees.

Some people try to test the A.I. assistants with unusual requests. For example, people are curious what else the assistants can do and ask for help in booking hotels, flights or conference rooms (things they can't do). Others ask Amy's age, or Andrew's birthday. "How do we elegantly recover when Amy or Andrew don't know what to do?" Ms. Kim said.

X.ai doesn't pretend the assistants are human. But Ms. Kim still gets satisfaction when people don't realize that the assistants are robots. People ask them out on dates. They receive thank-you emails from happy customers even though, as robots, they don't need gratitude.

"They're shocked and surprised that they were talking to an A.I.," she said.

'A CESSPOOL OF LEGAL LANGUAGE'

Dan Rubins, chief executive

Mr. Rubins has a lot of grievances with lawyers.

At his former job, he recalled the time when six corporate lawyers, each billing at hundreds of dollars an hour, were inspecting a contract looking for capitalization errors. It's what prompted him to create Legal Robot, a start-up that uses artificial intelligence to translate legalese into plain English.

Having reviewed nearly a million legal documents, Legal Robot also flags anomalies (strange wording or clauses) in contracts. "Lawyers have had 400 years to innovate and change the profession, and they haven't done it," said Mr. Rubins, who is not a lawyer. "It's time for some outside help."

He said legal documents are well suited to machine learning because they are highly structured and repetitive. Legal Robot tapped a vast trove of contracts prepared by human lawyers in filings with the Securities and Exchange Commission — "a cesspool of legal language," Mr. Rubins said — as well as past documents from law firms who wanted to help train Legal Robot's systems.

After going through a large set of documents, the company's machine learning systems start to recognize patterns indicating the words that tend to go together and those that do not. However, Mr. Rubins becomes worried when the A.I. is too confident about its results. That's often a byproduct of training the computer on too narrow a set of contracts.

For example, Legal Robot trained its A.I. on thousands of employment contracts from a state that allows noncompete clauses, which restrict employees from switching to a rival company. That meant when the A.I. saw contracts from states where noncompetes aren't enforceable, it nevertheless piped up to say the clause was missing. In other words, the A.I. was missing important context.

Mr. Rubins, 33, said the A.I. is good at identifying potentially vague word choices. He recently received a two-page nondisclosure agreement — it was reviewed by human lawyers — from another company containing the word "shall" 30 times. The A.I. pointed out that "shall" can be vague and advised that "will" or "may" are more clear, depending on the context.

Mr. Rubins doesn't think A.I. will put lawyers out of business, but it may change how they work and make money. The less time they need to spend reviewing contracts, the more time they can spend on, say, advisory work or litigation.

"I really don't think we're going to get rid of lawyers," he said. "Unfortunately, we still need them."

'THAT WAS A 'WOW' MOMENT FOR ME'

Sarah Seiwert, customer representative

It took two weeks for Ms. Seiwert to notice that her company's A.I. computer system was starting to pick up on her work patterns.

Ms. Seiwert, 37, a customer representative at the online test-prep company Magoosh, answers student emails. When a question comes in, she searches a database of preapproved responses and finds the appropriate answer.

There are thousands of different responses. Finding the right answer isn't as easy as it sounds.

When Magoosh implemented an A.I. system in February to help its customer service team work more efficiently, Ms. Seiwert noticed that it was reading the questions and suggesting responses.

If the suggestions were good, she would add a few niceties and send back a quick reply. But within two weeks, she noticed that even when she wasn't responding directly to an email, but following up to one that she had sent earlier, the software was suggesting the proper response.

"That was a 'wow' moment for me," said Ms. Seiwert, who works from a home office in Mankato, Minn. "It's been studying and learning my patterns."

As more customer service moves from phone calls to text-based conversations through chat or email, companies are looking to machine learning to help the human agents work faster. Magoosh is using software created by DigitalGenius, a London-based start-up.

When an email comes into Magoosh, the system reads the email, categorizes it and routes it to the appropriate employee. After a few months, some DigitalGenius customers start to automate responses for some common questions. Basically, this happens when the A.I. has seen enough examples of how human agents handled the request that it gains confidence that its answer will be correct.

Magoosh isn't there yet. But Ms. Seiwert said the software has reduced Magoosh's queue of customer requests by half, and it has made her team's goal of responding to every customer within 24 hours more manageable.

Even though the A.I. is learning from the human agents, Ms. Seiwert said she doesn't foresee a future where she's out of a job. Too many questions still require a level of human intuition to know the appropriate answer. There are also times when rules need to be broken, like when customers ask for an extension on their account because of some circumstance beyond their control.

"I am not convinced that artificial intelligence is going to replace us," she said. "You can't program intuition, a gut instinct. So the A.I. might get very intelligent, but I hope as a human I continue to get intelligent and not stand at a standstill."

THE 'CASES WE HAVEN'T SEEN BEFORE'

Aleksandra Faust, software engineer

As a senior software engineer at the self-driving car company Waymo and a robotics expert, Ms. Faust grapples with an unpredictable world.

Formerly known as Google's self-driving car project, Waymo wants to build autonomous vehicles that can react properly under all kinds of unusual circumstances. Not only when drivers run red lights, but also when a child crosses an intersection riding a hoverboard while walking a dog (which happened recently).

Waymo's cars have driven two million miles in the real world and billions more in computer simulations. But it's impossible to program for every event.

"There's always going to be some cases that we haven't seen before," Ms. Faust said. "Based on the situations it's seen, the A.I. helps the car react in situations it hasn't seen."

Safety is a concern, said Ms. Faust, 43, but so is comfort. Take the process of braking at a red light. When human drivers see a red light, they tend to slow down gradually before coming to a full stop. Waymo's driverless car was hitting the brake too abruptly in a way that human drivers would do if they weren't paying attention.

However, a sudden stop is dangerous because other drivers may not be paying attention. And it is jarring for the passengers.

Using real-world examples of how human drivers slow to a stop from different speeds, Ms. Faust's team creates different models for the most natural way a car should brake depending on how fast it is going. "One thing we've learned about human driving is that it's very, very complex," said Ms. Faust, who joined Waymo two years ago when it was still part of Google's research lab, X.

The Real Threat of Artificial Intelligence

OPINION | BY KAI-FU LEE | JUNE 24, 2017

BEIJING — What worries you about the coming world of artificial intelligence?

Too often the answer to this question resembles the plot of a sci-fi thriller. People worry that developments in A.I. will bring about the "singularity" — that point in history when A.I. surpasses human intelligence, leading to an unimaginable revolution in human affairs. Or they wonder whether instead of our controlling artificial intelligence, it will control us, turning us, in effect, into cyborgs.

These are interesting issues to contemplate, but they are not pressing. They concern situations that may not arise for hundreds of years, if ever. At the moment, there is no known path from our best A.I. tools (like the Google computer program that recently beat the world's best player of the game of Go) to "general" A.I. — self-aware computer programs that can engage in common-sense reasoning, attain knowledge in multiple domains, feel, express and understand emotions and so on.

This doesn't mean we have nothing to worry about. On the contrary, the A.I. products that now exist are improving faster than most people realize and promise to radically transform our world, not always for the better. They are only tools, not a competing form of intelligence. But they will reshape what work means and how wealth is created, leading to unprecedented economic inequalities and even altering the global balance of power.

It is imperative that we turn our attention to these imminent challenges.

What is artificial intelligence today? Roughly speaking, it's technology that takes in huge amounts of information from a specific domain (say, loan repayment histories) and uses it to make a decision in a specific case (whether to give an individual a loan) in the service of a specified goal (maximizing profits for the lender). Think of a spreadsheet on steroids, trained on big data. These tools can outperform human beings at a given task.

This kind of A.I. is spreading to thousands of domains (not just loans), and as it does, it will eliminate many jobs. Bank tellers, customer service representatives, telemarketers, stock and bond traders, even paralegals and radiologists will gradually be replaced by such software. Over time this technology will come to control semiautonomous and autonomous hardware like self-driving cars and robots, displacing factory workers, construction workers, drivers, delivery workers and many others.

Unlike the Industrial Revolution and the computer revolution, the A.I. revolution is not taking certain jobs (artisans, personal assistants who use paper and typewriters) and replacing them with other jobs (assembly-line workers, personal assistants conversant with computers). Instead, it is poised to bring about a wide-scale decimation of jobs — mostly lower-paying jobs, but some higher-paying ones, too.

This transformation will result in enormous profits for the companies that develop A.I., as well as for the companies that adopt it. Imagine how much money a company like Uber would make if it used only robot drivers. Imagine the profits if Apple could manufacture its products without human labor. Imagine the gains to a loan company that could issue 30 million loans a year with virtually no human involvement. (As it happens, my venture capital firm has invested in just such a loan company.)

We are thus facing two developments that do not sit easily together: enormous wealth concentrated in relatively few hands and enormous numbers of people out of work. What is to be done?

Part of the answer will involve educating or retraining people in tasks A.I. tools aren't good at. Artificial intelligence is poorly suited for jobs involving creativity, planning and "cross-domain" thinking — for example, the work of a trial lawyer. But these skills are typically required by high-paying jobs that may be hard to retrain displaced workers to do. More promising are lower-paying jobs involving the "people skills" that A.I. lacks: social workers, bartenders, concierges — professions requiring nuanced human interaction. But here, too, there is a problem: How many bartenders does a society really need?

The solution to the problem of mass unemployment, I suspect, will involve "service jobs of love." These are jobs that A.I. cannot do, that society needs and that give people a sense of purpose. Examples include accompanying an older person to visit a doctor, mentoring at an orphanage and serving as a sponsor at Alcoholics Anonymous — or, potentially soon, Virtual Reality Anonymous (for those addicted to their parallel lives in computer-generated simulations). The volunteer service jobs of today, in other words, may turn into the real jobs of the future.

Other volunteer jobs may be higher-paying and professional, such as compassionate medical service providers who serve as the "human interface" for A.I. programs that diagnose cancer. In all cases, people will be able to choose to work fewer hours than they do now.

Who will pay for these jobs? Here is where the enormous wealth concentrated in relatively few hands comes in. It strikes me as unavoidable that large chunks of the money created by A.I. will have to be transferred to those whose jobs have been displaced. This seems feasible only through Keynesian policies of increased government spending, presumably raised through taxation on wealthy companies.

As for what form that social welfare would take, I would argue for a conditional universal basic income: welfare offered to those who have a financial need, on the condition they either show an effort to receive training that would make them employable or commit to a certain number of hours of "service of love" voluntarism.

To fund this, tax rates will have to be high. The government will not only have to subsidize most people's lives and work; it will also have to compensate for the loss of individual tax revenue previously collected from employed individuals. This leads to the final and perhaps most consequential challenge of A.I. The Keynesian approach I have sketched out may be feasible in the United States and China, which will have enough successful A.I. businesses to fund welfare initiatives via taxes. But what about other countries?

They face two insurmountable problems. First, most of the money being made from artificial intelligence will go to the United States and China. A.I. is an industry in which strength begets strength: The more data you have, the better your product; the better your product, the more data you can collect; the more data you can collect, the more talent you can attract; the more talent you can attract, the better your product. It's a virtuous circle, and the United States and China have already amassed the talent, market share and data to set it in motion.

For example, the Chinese speech-recognition company iFlytek and several Chinese face-recognition companies such as Megvii and SenseTime have become industry leaders, as measured by market capitalization. The United States is spearheading the development of autonomous vehicles, led by companies like Google, Tesla and Uber. As for the consumer internet market, seven American or Chinese companies — Google, Facebook, Microsoft, Amazon, Baidu, Alibaba and Tencent — are making extensive use of A.I. and expanding operations to other countries, essentially owning those A.I. markets. It seems American businesses will dominate in developed markets and some developing markets, while Chinese companies will win in most developing markets.

The other challenge for many countries that are not China or the United States is that their populations are increasing, especially in the developing world. While a large, growing population can be an economic asset (as in China and India in recent decades), in the age of A.I. it will be an economic liability because it will comprise mostly displaced workers, not productive ones.

So if most countries will not be able to tax ultra-profitable A.I. companies to subsidize their workers, what options will they have? I foresee only one: Unless they wish to plunge their people into poverty, they will be forced to negotiate with whichever country supplies most of their A.I. software — China or the United States — to essentially become that country's economic dependent, taking in welfare subsidies in exchange for letting the "parent" nation's A.I. companies continue to profit from the dependent country's users. Such economic arrangements would reshape today's geopolitical alliances.

One way or another, we are going to have to start thinking about how to minimize the looming A.I.-fueled gap between the haves and the have-nots, both within and between nations. Or to put the matter more optimistically: A.I. is presenting us with an opportunity to rethink economic inequality on a global scale. These challenges are too far-ranging in their effects for any nation to isolate itself from the rest of the world.

KAI-FU LEE is the chairman and chief executive of Sinovation Ventures, a venture capital firm, and the president of its Artificial Intelligence Institute.

A.I. Will Transform the Economy. But How Much, and How Soon?

BY STEVE LOHR | NOV. 30, 2017

THERE ARE BASICALLY three big questions about artificial intelligence and its impact on the economy: What can it do? Where is it headed? And how fast will it spread?

Three new reports combine to suggest these answers: It can probably do less right now than you think. But it will eventually do more than you probably think, in more places than you probably think, and will probably evolve faster than powerful technologies have in the past.

This bundle of research is itself a sign of the A.I. boom. Researchers across disciplines are scrambling to understand the likely trajectory, reach and influence of the technology — already finding its way into things like self-driving cars and image recognition online — in all its dimensions. Doing so raises a host of challenges of definition and measurement, because the field is moving quickly — and because companies are branding things A.I. for marketing purposes.

An "AI Index," created by researchers at Stanford University, the Massachusetts Institute of Technology and other organizations, released on Thursday, tracks developments in artificial intelligence by measuring aspects like technical progress, investment, research citations and university enrollments. The goal of the project is to collect, curate and continually update data to better inform scientists, businesspeople, policymakers and the public.

The McKinsey Global Institute published a report on Wednesday about automation and jobs, sketching out different paths the technology might take and its effect on workers, by job category in several countries. One finding: Up to one third of the American work force will have to switch to new occupations by 2030, in about a dozen years.

And in an article published in November by the National Bureau of Economic Research, economists from M.I.T. and the University of Chicago suggest an answer to the puzzle of why all the research and investment in A.I. technology have so far had little effect on productivity.

Each of the three research initiatives has a somewhat different focus. But two common themes emerge from the reports and interviews with their authors.

- Technology itself is only one ingredient in determining the trajectory of A.I. and its influence. Economics, government policy and social attitudes will play major roles as well.

- Historical patterns of adoption of major technologies, from electricity to computers, are likely to hold true for A.I. But if the pattern is similar, the pace may not be. And if it is much faster, as many researchers predict, the social consequences could be far more wrenching than in past transitions.

The AI Index grew out of the One Hundred Year Study on Artificial Intelligence, a Stanford-based project begun in 2014 by A.I. experts. The study group, mainly scientists, seeks to broaden understanding of artificial intelligence and thus increase the odds society will be benefit from the technology.

The group was initially going to publish major studies every five years. But given the speed of progress and investment, the five-year interval "seemed way too slow," said Yoav Shoham, a professor emeritus at Stanford and chair of the steering committee for the "AI Index."

The new index is not a single number, but a series of charts and graphs that track A.I.-related trends over time. They include measures like the rate of improvement in image identification and speech recognition, as well as start-up activity and job openings. There are also short essays by artificial intelligence experts.

Some of the charts showing the progress of technology are telling. Image and speech recognition programs, for example, have matched or surpassed human capabilities in just the past year or two.

But A.I. experts warn that gains in specific tasks or game-playing proficiency are still a far cry from general intelligence. A child, for example, knows that a water glass tipping on the edge of a table will most likely fall to the floor and spill the water. He or she understands the physics of everyday life in a way artificial intelligence programs do not yet.

"The public thinks we know how to do far more than we do now," said Raymond Perrault, a scientist at SRI International, who worked on the index.

The current "AI Index," Mr. Shoham said, is "very much a first step." The group is seeking contributions of data and comments from academic and corporate researchers around the world. The idea, he said, is to create "a living index" that details as many measurable dimensions of the field as possible, including social impact.

The McKinsey automation-and-jobs report captures the uncertainty surrounding A.I. and its coming effect on labor markets. Its projection of the number of Americans who will have to find new occupations by 2030 ranges from 16 million to 54 million — depending on the pace of technology adoption.

The faster A.I. advances, the greater the challenge. McKinsey's upper-range projection of 54 million suggests a more rapid transformation than in previous waves of change in the work force, when employment migrated from farms to factories and later from manufacturing to services.

"That's where the conversation has to go — how to manage this transition," said Susan Lund, an economist at McKinsey. "We need a major change in how we provide midcareer retraining and how we help displaced workers find new employment."

Still, the rise of A.I. has not yet shown up in the economy as a whole, at least not in the numbers. In their recent paper, Erik Brynjolfsson and Daniel Rock of the M.I.T. Sloan School of Management and Chad Syverson of the University of Chicago Booth School of Business call it "a clash of expectations and statistics."

They offer a few possible explanations, including false hopes and poor measurements of the new technology. But the one they settle on is a lag in the adoption and effective use of A.I.

There are historical precedents. The electric motor, for example, was introduced in the early 1880s. But it was not until the 1920s that discernible productivity gains showed up, after the motors spread and factory work was reorganized into mass-production assembly lines to exploit the new technology of its day.

A.I. will follow a similar path, but faster, predicts Mr. Brynjolfsson, who also worked in the "AI Index." And the index, he said, should help accelerate adoption by giving people needed information to make better decisions.

There are A.I. skeptics, but Mr. Brynjolfsson is not one of them. "History shows it takes years, even with a powerful technology in place," he said. "But to me, it's dead certain it's going to happen."

Will Robots Take Our Children's Jobs?

BY ALEX WILLIAMS | DEC. 11, 2017

LIKE A LOT OF CHILDREN, my sons, Toby, 7, and Anton, 4, are obsessed with robots. In the children's books they devour at bedtime, happy, helpful robots pop up more often than even dragons or dinosaurs. The other day I asked Toby why children like robots so much.

"Because they work for you," he said.

What I didn't have the heart to tell him is, someday he might work for them — or, I fear, might not work at all, because of them.

It is not just Elon Musk, Bill Gates and Stephen Hawking who are freaking out about the rise of invincible machines. Yes, robots have the potential to outsmart us and destroy the human race. But first, artificial intelligence could make countless professions obsolete by the time my sons reach their 20s.

You do not exactly need to be Marty McFly to see the obvious threats to our children's future careers.

Say you dream of sending your daughter off to Yale School of Medicine to become a radiologist. And why not? Radiologists in New York typically earn about $470,000, according to Salary.com.

But that job is suddenly looking iffy as A.I. gets better at reading scans. A start-up called Arterys, to cite just one example, already has a program that can perform a magnetic-resonance imaging analysis of blood flow through a heart in just 15 seconds, compared with the 45 minutes required by humans.

Maybe she wants to be a surgeon, but that job may not be safe, either. Robots already assist surgeons in removing damaged organs and cancerous tissue, according to Scientific American. Last year, a prototype robotic surgeon called STAR (Smart Tissue Autonomous Robot) outperformed human surgeons in a test in which both had to repair the severed intestine of a live pig.

So perhaps your daughter detours to law school to become a rainmaking corporate lawyer. Skies are cloudy in that profession, too. Any legal job that involves lots of mundane document review (and that's a lot of what lawyers do) is vulnerable.

Software programs are already being used by companies including JPMorgan Chase & Company to scan legal papers and predict what documents are relevant, saving lots of billable hours. Kira Systems, for example, has reportedly cut the time that some lawyers need to review contracts by 20 to 60 percent.

As a matter of professional survival, I would like to assure my children that journalism is immune, but that is clearly a delusion. The Associated Press already has used a software program from a company called Automated Insights to churn out passable copy covering Wall Street earnings and some college sports, and last year awarded the bots the minor league baseball beat.

What about other glamour jobs, like airline pilot? Well, last spring, a robotic co-pilot developed by the Defense Advanced Research Projects Agency, known as Darpa, flew and landed a simulated 737. I hardly count that as surprising, given that pilots of commercial Boeing 777s, according to one 2015 survey, only spend seven minutes during an average flight actually flying the thing. As we move into the era of driverless cars, can pilotless planes be far behind?

Then there is Wall Street, where robots are already doing their best to shove Gordon Gekko out of his corner office. Big banks are using software programs that can suggest bets, construct hedges and act as robo-economists, using natural language processing to parse central bank commentary to predict monetary policy, according to Bloomberg. BlackRock, the biggest fund company in the world, made waves earlier this year when it announced it was replacing some highly paid human stock pickers with computer algorithms.

So am I paranoid? Or not paranoid enough? A much-quoted 2013 study by the University of Oxford Department of Engineering Science — surely the most sober of institutions — estimated that 47 percent of current jobs, including insurance underwriter, sports referee and loan officer, are at risk of falling victim to automation, perhaps within a decade or two.

Just this week, the McKinsey Global Institute released a report that found that a third of American workers may have to switch jobs in the next dozen or so years because of A.I.

I know I am not the only parent wondering if I can robot-proof my children's careers. I figured I would start by asking my own what they want to do when they grow up.

Toby, a people pleaser and born entertainer, is obsessed with cars and movies. He told me he wanted to be either an Uber driver or an actor. (He is too young to understand that those jobs are usually one and the same).

As for Uber drivers, it is no secret that they are headed to that great parking garage in the sky; the company recently announced plans to buy 24,000 Volvo sport utility vehicles to roll out as a driverless fleet between 2019 and 2021.

And actors? It may seem unthinkable that some future computer-generated thespian could achieve the nuance of expression and emotional depth of, say, Dwayne Johnson. But Hollywood is already Silicon Valley South. Consider how filmmakers used computer graphics to reanimate Carrie Fisher's Princess Leia and Peter Cushing's Grand Moff Tarkin as they appeared in the 1970s (never mind that Mr. Cushing died in 1994) for "Rogue One: A Star Wars Story."

My younger son Anton, a sweetheart, but tough as Kevlar, said he wanted to be a football player. Robot football may sound crazy, but come to think of it, a Monday night battle between the Dallas Cowdroids and Seattle Seabots may be the only solution to the sport's endless concussion problems.

He also said he wanted to be a soldier. If he means foot soldier, however, he might want to hold off on enlistment. Russia recently unveiled Fedor, a humanoid robot soldier that looks like RoboCop after a Whole30 crash diet; this space-combat-ready android can fire handguns, drive vehicles, administer first aid and, one hopes, salute. Indeed, the world's armies are in such an arms race developing grunt-bots that one British intelligence expert predicted that American forces will have more robot soldiers than humans by 2025.

And again, all of this stuff is happening now, not 25 years from now. Who knows what the jobs marketplace might look like by then. We might not even be the smartest beings on the planet.

Ever heard of the "singularity"? That is the term that futurists use to describe a potentially cataclysmic point at which machine intelligence catches up to human intelligence, and likely blows right past it. They may rule us. They may kill us. No wonder Mr. Musk says that A.I. "is potentially more dangerous than nukes."

But is it really that dire? Fears of technology are as old as the Luddites, those machine-smashing British textile workers of the early 19th century. Usually, the fears turn out to be overblown.

The rise of the automobile, to cite the obvious example, did indeed put most manure shovelers out of work. But it created millions of jobs to replace them, not just for Detroit assembly line workers, but for suburban homebuilders, Big Mac flippers and actors performing "Greased Lightnin' " in touring revivals of "Grease." That is the process of creative destruction in a nutshell.

But artificial intelligence is different, said Martin Ford, the author of "Rise of the Robots: Technology and the Threat of a Jobless Future." Machine learning does not just give us new machines to replace old machines, pushing human workers from one industry to another. Rather, it gives us new machines to replace us, machines that can follow us to virtually any new industry we flee to.

Since Mr. Ford's book sent me down this rabbit hole in the first place, I reached out to him to see if he was concerned about all this for his own children: Tristan, 22, Colin, 17, and Elaine, 10.

He said the most vulnerable jobs in the robot economy are those involving predictable, repetitive tasks, however much training they require. "A lot of knowledge-based jobs are really routine — sitting in front of a computer and cranking out the same application over and over, whether it is a report or some kind of quantitative analysis," he said.

Professions that rely on creative thinking enjoy some protection (Mr. Ford's older son is a graduate student studying biomedical engineering). So do jobs emphasizing empathy and interpersonal communication (his younger son wants to be a psychologist).

Even so, the ability to think creatively may not provide ultimate salvation. Mr. Ford said he was alarmed in May when Google's AlphaGo software defeated a 19-year-old Chinese master at Go, considered the world's most complicated board game.

"If you talk to the best Go players, even they can't explain what they're doing," Mr. Ford said. "They'll describe it as a 'feeling.' It's moving into the realm of intuition. And yet a computer was able to prove that it can beat anyone in the world."

Looking for a silver lining, I spent an afternoon Googling TED Talks with catchy titles like "Are Droids Taking Our Jobs?"

In one, Albert Wenger, an influential tech investor, promoted the Basic Income Guarantee concept. Also known as Universal Basic Income, this sunny concept holds that a robot-driven economy may someday produce an unlimited bounty of cool stuff while simultaneously releasing us from the drudgery of old-fashioned labor, leaving our government-funded children to enjoy bountiful lives of leisure as interpretive dancers or practitioners of bee-sting therapy, as touted by Gwyneth Paltrow.

The idea is all the rage among Silicon Valley elites, who not only understand technology's power, but who also love to believe that it will be used for good. In their vision of a post-A.I. world without traditional jobs, everyone will receive a minimum weekly or monthly stipend (welfare for all, basically).

Another talk by David Autor, an economist, argued that reports of the death of work are greatly exaggerated. Almost 50 years after the introduction of the A.T.M., for instance, more humans actually work as bank tellers than ever. The computers simply freed the humans from mind-numbing work like counting out 20-dollar bills to focus on more cognitively demanding tasks like "forging relationships with customers, solving problems and introducing them to new products like credit cards, loans and investments," he said.

Computers, after all, are really good at some things and, for the moment, terrible at others. Even Anton intuits this. The other day I asked him if he thought robots were smarter or dumber than humans. "Sdumber," he said after a long pause. Confused, I pushed him. "Smarter and dumber," he explained with a cheeky smile.

He was joking. But he also happened to be right, according to Andrew McAfee, a management theorist at the Massachusetts Institute of Technology whom I interviewed a short while later.

Discussing another of Anton's career aspirations — songwriter — Dr. McAfee said that computers were already smart enough to come up with a better melody than a lot of humans. "The things our ears find pleasant, we know the rules for that stuff," he said. "However, I'm going to be really surprised when there is a digital lyricist out there, somebody who can put words to that music that will actually resonate with people and make them think something about the human condition."

Not everyone, of course, is cut out to be a cyborg-Springsteen. I asked Dr. McAfee what other jobs may exist a decade from now.

"I think health coaches are going to be a big industry of the future," he said. "Restaurants that have a very good hospitality staff are not about to go away, even though we have more options to order via tablet.

"People who are interested in working with their hands, they're going to be fine," he said. "The robot plumber is a long, long way away."

A.I. and Big Data Could Power a New War on Poverty

OPINION | BY ELISABETH A. MASON | JAN. 1, 2018

WHEN IT COMES to artificial intelligence and jobs, the prognostications are grim. The conventional wisdom is that A.I. might soon put millions of people out of work — that it stands poised to do to clerical and white collar workers over the next two decades what mechanization did to factory workers over the past two. And that is to say nothing of the truckers and taxi drivers who will find themselves unemployed or underemployed as self-driving cars take over our roads.

But it's time we start thinking about A.I.'s potential benefits for society as well as its drawbacks. The big-data and A.I. revolutions could also help fight poverty and promote economic stability.

Poverty, of course, is a multifaceted phenomenon. But the condition of poverty often entails one or more of these realities: a lack of income (joblessness); a lack of preparedness (education); and a dependency on government services (welfare). A.I. can address all three.

First, even as A.I. threatens to put people out of work, it can simultaneously be used to match them to good middle-class jobs that are going unfilled. Today there are millions of such jobs in the United States. This is precisely the kind of matching problem at which A.I. excels. Likewise, A.I. can predict where the job openings of tomorrow will lie, and which skills and training will be needed for them.

Historically we have tended to shy away from this kind of social planning and job matching, perhaps because it smacks to us of a command economy. No one, however, is suggesting that the government should force workers to train for and accept particular jobs — or indeed that identifying these jobs and skills gaps needs to be the work of the government. The point is that we now have the tools to take the guesswork out of which jobs are available and which skills workers need to fill them.

Second, we can bring what is known as differentiated education — based on the idea that students master skills in different ways and at different speeds — to every student in the country. A 2013 study by Indian researchers found that nearly 40 percent of medical students held a strong preference for one mode of learning: Some were listeners; others were visual learners; still others learned best by doing.

Our school system effectively assumes precisely the opposite. We bundle students into a room, use the same method of instruction and hope for the best. A.I. can improve this state of affairs. Even within the context of a standardized curriculum, A.I. "tutors" can home in on and correct for each student's weaknesses, adapt coursework to his or her learning style and keep the student engaged.

Today's dominant type of A.I., also known as machine learning, permits computer programs to become more accurate — to learn, if you will — as they absorb data and correlate it with known examples from other data sets. In this way, the A.I. "tutor" becomes increasingly effective at matching a student's needs as it spends more time seeing what works to improve performance.

Third, a concerted effort to drag education and job training and matching into the 21st century ought to remove the reliance of a substantial portion of the population on government programs designed to assist struggling Americans. With 21st-century technology, we could plausibly reduce the use of government assistance services to levels where they serve the function for which they were originally intended.

Big data sets can now be harnessed to better predict which programs help certain people at a given time and to quickly assess whether programs are having the desired effect. To use an advertising analogy, this would be the difference between placing a commercial on prime-time television and doing so through micro-targeted analytics. Guess which one is cheaper and better able to reach the target population?

As for the poisonous effect of ideology on the debate over public assistance: Big data promises something closer to an unbiased, ideology-free evaluation of the effectiveness of these social programs.

We could come closer to the vision of a meritocratic, technocratic society that politicians from both parties at state and local levels — those closest to the practical problems their constituents face — have begun to embrace.

Even Congress occasionally wakes up from its partisan slumber to advance the cause of technology in public policy decision-making: In 2016, Congress voted for and President Barack Obama authorized the creation of the Commission on Evidence-Based Policy Making. The act creating the commission was sponsored by Senator Patty Murray, a Democrat, and Paul Ryan, the House speaker. Before the commission expired in September 2017, it used government data to evaluate the effectiveness of government policy and made recommendations based on its findings.

This provides one more indication of the promise of A.I. and big data in the service of positive, purposeful public good. Before we dismiss these new technologies as nothing more than agents of chaos and disruption, we ought to consider their potential to work to society's advantage.

ELISABETH A. MASON is the founding director of the Stanford Poverty and Technology Lab and a senior adviser at the Stanford Center on Poverty and Inequality.

A.I. Has Arrived in Investing. Humans Are Still Dominating.

BY CONRAD DE AENLLE | JAN. 12, 2018

MACHINES ARE STARTING to take the place of the people who flip burgers, drive across town and, lately, manage stock portfolios.

Artificial intelligence is taking on a bigger role in making investment decisions.

A.I., including an ability to analyze data and actually learn from it, is considered useful in executing certain investing models, such as high-frequency trading, and in helping fund managers with tasks that rely on gathering and interpreting reams of information. Going a step further, an exchange-traded fund introduced in October uses A.I. algorithms to choose long-term stock holdings.

It is too early to say whether the E.T.F., A.I. Powered Equity, will be a trendsetter or merely a curiosity. Artificial intelligence continues to become more sophisticated and complex, but so do the markets. That leaves technology and investment authorities debating the role of A.I. in managing portfolios. Some say it will only ever be a tool, valuable but subordinate to its flesh-and-blood masters, while others envision it taking control and making decisions for many funds.

"We are just beginning to see a rise of the machines in investment management," said Campbell Harvey, a professor of finance at Duke University. Although, he said, "it's hard to define what the markets will look like" if human judgment is usurped, he predicted that "in the end, it will be a good thing for investors."

Artificial intelligence is a term that may be spoken more than understood. Many investment firms use software to sift through data and perform rudimentary analysis by following fairly simple rules. The programs can create portfolios by screening universes of stocks to select ones that meet criteria related to corporate results, valuation metrics or trading patterns, or by tweaking the proportions of the constituent companies in an index based on certain factors.

Those programs may be useful, but they are not A.I. because they are static; they do the same thing over and over until someone changes them. A.I. involves machine learning, in which a program updates itself as new information comes in. Whatever goal the program was created to achieve remains the same, but the problem-solving tools it uses keep changing and reflect the sum of the information it has to work with.

Large fund management companies like Fidelity and Vanguard say they use A.I. for a range of purposes, but they decline to be specific.

BlackRock says it relies on it for heavy cognitive lifting, often by scouring data to tease out patterns that might remain obscure to human eyes and brains. Examples offered by Jessica Greaney, a company spokeswoman, include identifying and trying to exploit nonintuitive relationships between securities or market indicators, perusing social media "to gain insights on employee attitudes, sentiment and preferences," and monitoring search engines for words being entered on particular topics, say cars or luxury goods.

These algorithms play a supporting role in BlackRock's investing, Ms. Greaney said. Decisions on what to buy and sell are made by living, breathing managers.

The A.I. Powered Equity E.T.F. is different. It uses algorithms to go the last mile and select its holdings, usually 30 to 70 stocks, said Art Amador, one of the founders of EquBot, the company that created the fund. He had the assistance of an I.B.M. program that fosters technology start-ups, and the E.T.F. runs most of its calculations on I.B.M.'s Watson supercomputer.

"EquBot's A.I. tech mimics the investment process of an army of equity research analysts working around the clock," Mr. Amador said. "It has data on 6,000 companies, one million articles and filings a day, and data on market sentiment." Beyond sorting through that information and using its programming to ensure it has what it

CHRISTIE HEMM KLOK FOR THE NEW YORK TIMES

Art Amador, one of the founders of EquBot, in San Francisco.

considers the optimal portfolio — the fund typically makes at least one trade every day — it constantly fine-tunes its stock-picking methods.

Mr. Amador says that artificial intelligence has an edge over the natural kind because of the inherent emotional and psychological weaknesses that encumber human reasoning.

"When it comes to traditional portfolio management, managers are going to talk to analysts and sector specialists, but these people have biases and incentives," he said. "The algorithm doesn't have them."

What it also doesn't have is a superior track record. Between Oct. 18, when it began trading, and the end of the year, the E.T.F. rose 3.1 percent, compared with a 5.1 percent gain for the Standard & Poor's 500-stock index.

Mr. Amador attributed the underperformance to a normal variability in returns. The fund's programming beat the market when tested against historical data, he said, and he expects the same in real life as time passes.

Others aren't so sure how effective A.I. will be when put in charge of otherwise ordinary funds. Robert Arnott, chairman of the investment firm Research Affiliates, noted that A.I. can process immense amounts of data; the flip side is that it needs immense amounts of data for the algorithms to learn.

Certain activities, like high-frequency trading, process market information tick by tick and seek to profit from making numerous trades and holding positions for matters of hours or minutes. Compared with conventional investing, this sort of trading gives A.I. programs more data, Mr. Arnott said, but it is limited in scope to patterns related to stock price movements, not the broader economic and commercial landscape.

When it comes to managing long-term portfolios, however, there are too many moving parts in financial markets for A.I. to get its mechanical head around, in his view, and too many humans with flaws, motivations and unpredictable behavior doing the moving. He says the markets are far more complex than the games like chess and backgammon that A.I. algorithms have mastered.

Tim Clift, chief investment strategist at Envestnet PMC, a firm that helps build portfolios, said that while artificial intelligence can give managers an edge, it is "a little gimmicky at this point."

"We know the markets are irrational, especially in the short term," he said, "but the machines aren't going to know how to behave in that kind of environment."

Gregg Fisher, a portfolio manager at the Gerstein Fisher Funds, cautioned that A.I. programs could be stumped by off-the-wall and out-of-the-blue developments that have no obvious analogues in their databases.

They learn "by studying past patterns that they expect to continue," he said. Referring to the events that precipitated the global financial crisis, he wondered: "How would A.I. have observed and planned for that? The quantity of different things that can happen is seemingly unlimited."

But for advocates of A.I., like Mr. Harvey at Duke, the ability to gather data and put it to good use also seems to be unlimited. He expects great strides in machine learning in the decades to come, allowing A.I. to assume a major role in how funds are managed and by whom.

"Larger firms will be providing information to managers that other firms have no chance of getting" because they can't afford the necessary data management systems, he said. The result will be "15 to 25 investment management superpowers that can harvest all that data."

Maybe so, but some investment professionals prefer to give the final say to portfolio managers who were born, not made.

"I'm a fan of automating everything possible, but having a human being push the last button is still a good thing," Mr. Fisher said. "Hopefully, we all get better and better and smarter and smarter, but there's something comforting about having an informed human being with sound judgment at the end of the process."

Most Americans See Artificial Intelligence as a Threat to Jobs (Just Not Theirs)

BY NIRAJ CHOKSHI | MARCH 6, 2018

THE VAST MAJORITY of Americans expect artificial intelligence to lead to job losses in the coming decade, but few see it coming for their own position.

And despite the expected decline in employment, the public widely embraces artificial intelligence in attitude and in practice. About five in six Americans already use a product or service that features it, according to a survey that was conducted last fall and from which new findings were released on Tuesday.

"Whether they know it or not, A.I. has moved into a big percent of Americans' lives in one way or another already," said Frank Newport, the editor in chief of Gallup, which conducted the survey with Northeastern University.

The study defines artificial intelligence as any technology that can perform a task as humans do. But even if that definition feels overly broad, the findings reveal just how ubiquitous certain products have become in American life.

About 84 percent of Americans, for example, use navigation apps like Google Maps, Waze and Apple Maps, the study found. About 72 percent of respondents said they streamed music or video with services like Netflix and Pandora.

Nearly half said they used personal assistants on their smartphones, while about 32 percent use ride-sharing apps. Some 22 percent used intelligent home personal assistants, like Google Home or Amazon's Alexa. Twenty percent said they use a smart home device, such as a self-learning light or thermostat.

The technologies were used most widely among younger and more educated Americans: More than 90 percent of adults with at least a bachelor's degree or between the ages of 18 and 35 used navigation apps, for example.

The report that was released on Tuesday reflects only some of the findings of a large survey of nearly 3,300 American adults conducted in September and October.

The other findings, released in January, show that more than three in four Americans believe that artificial intelligence will fundamentally change how the public works and lives in the coming decade.

About the same share expect artificial intelligence to destroy more jobs than it creates, though only about one in four were worried about losing their own job.

CHAPTER 3

Artificial Anxiety

Attitudes about A.I. tend to take one of two positions: either strong A.I. will inaugurate unprecedented benefits to humanity or it will propel us into a dystopian nightmare. The contrast makes people anxious. A.I. may, for example, be harnessed by governments to make warfare more efficient and to increase the effectiveness of policing. These may be seen as welcome or frightening developments, depending on your point of view. A.I. might also reproduce the prejudices it inherits from its programmers and the data it uses. It may destroy all of us. Or only some of us. But it may not. How, then, do we make A.I. behave?

Scientists Worry Machines May Outsmart Man

BY JOHN MARKOFF | JULY 25, 2009

A ROBOT THAT can open doors and find electrical outlets to recharge itself. Computer viruses that no one can stop. Predator drones, which, though still controlled remotely by humans, come close to a machine that can kill autonomously.

Impressed and alarmed by advances in artificial intelligence, a group of computer scientists is debating whether there should be limits on research that might lead to loss of human control over computer-based systems that carry a growing share of society's workload, from waging war to chatting with customers on the phone.

Their concern is that further advances could create profound social disruptions and even have dangerous consequences.

As examples, the scientists pointed to a number of technologies as diverse as experimental medical systems that interact with patients to simulate empathy, and computer worms and viruses that defy extermination and could thus be said to have reached a "cockroach" stage of machine intelligence.

While the computer scientists agreed that we are a long way from Hal, the computer that took over the spaceship in "2001: A Space Odyssey," they said there was legitimate concern that technological progress would transform the work force by destroying a widening range of jobs, as well as force humans to learn to live with machines that increasingly copy human behaviors.

The researchers — leading computer scientists, artificial intelligence researchers and roboticists who met at the Asilomar Conference Grounds on Monterey Bay in California — generally discounted the possibility of highly centralized superintelligences and the idea that intelligence might spring spontaneously from the Internet. But they agreed that robots that can kill autonomously are either already here or will be soon.

They focused particular attention on the specter that criminals could exploit artificial intelligence systems as soon as they were developed. What could a criminal do with a speech synthesis system that could masquerade as a human being? What happens if artificial intelligence technology is used to mine personal information from smart phones?

The researchers also discussed possible threats to human jobs, like self-driving cars, software-based personal assistants and service robots in the home. Just last month, a service robot developed by Willow Garage in Silicon Valley proved it could navigate the real world.

A report from the conference, which took place in private on Feb. 25, is to be issued later this year. Some attendees discussed the meeting for the first time with other scientists this month and in interviews.

The conference was organized by the Association for the Advancement of Artificial Intelligence, and in choosing Asilomar for the discussions, the group purposefully evoked a landmark event in the history of science. In 1975, the world's leading biologists also met at Asilomar to discuss the new ability to reshape life by swapping genetic material among organisms. Concerned about possible biohazards and ethical questions, scientists had halted certain experiments. The conference led to guidelines for recombinant DNA research, enabling experimentation to continue.

The meeting on the future of artificial intelligence was organized by Eric Horvitz, a Microsoft researcher who is now president of the association.

Dr. Horvitz said he believed computer scientists must respond to the notions of superintelligent machines and artificial intelligence systems run amok.

The idea of an "intelligence explosion" in which smart machines would design even more intelligent machines was proposed by the mathematician I. J. Good in 1965. Later, in lectures and science fiction novels, the computer scientist Vernor Vinge popularized the notion of a moment when humans will create smarter-than-human machines, causing such rapid change that the "human era will be ended." He called this shift the Singularity.

This vision, embraced in movies and literature, is seen as plausible and unnerving by some scientists like William Joy, co-founder of Sun Microsystems. Other technologists, notably Raymond Kurzweil, have extolled the coming of ultrasmart machines, saying they will offer huge advances in life extension and wealth creation.

"Something new has taken place in the past five to eight years," Dr. Horvitz said. "Technologists are providing almost religious visions, and their ideas are resonating in some ways with the same idea of the Rapture."

The Kurzweil version of technological utopia has captured imaginations in Silicon Valley. This summer an organization called the Singularity University began offering courses to prepare a "cadre" to shape the advances and help society cope with the ramifications.

"My sense was that sooner or later we would have to make some sort of statement or assessment, given the rising voice of the technorati and people very concerned about the rise of intelligent machines," Dr. Horvitz said.

The A.A.A.I. report will try to assess the possibility of "the loss of human control of computer-based intelligences." It will also grapple, Dr. Horvitz said, with socioeconomic, legal and ethical issues, as well as probable changes in human-computer relationships. How would it be, for example, to relate to a machine that is as intelligent as your spouse?

Dr. Horvitz said the panel was looking for ways to guide research so that technology improved society rather than moved it toward a technological catastrophe. Some research might, for instance, be conducted in a high-security laboratory.

The meeting on artificial intelligence could be pivotal to the future of the field. Paul Berg, who was the organizer of the 1975 Asilomar meeting and received a Nobel Prize for chemistry in 1980, said it was important for scientific communities to engage the public before alarm and opposition becomes unshakable.

"If you wait too long and the sides become entrenched like with G.M.O.," he said, referring to genetically modified foods, "then it is very difficult. It's too complex, and people talk right past each other."

Tom Mitchell, a professor of artificial intelligence and machine learning at Carnegie Mellon University, said the February meeting had changed his thinking. "I went in very optimistic about the future of A.I. and thinking that Bill Joy and Ray Kurzweil were far off in their predictions," he said. But, he added, "The meeting made me want to be more outspoken about these issues and in particular be outspoken about the vast amounts of data collected about our personal lives."

Despite his concerns, Dr. Horvitz said he was hopeful that artificial intelligence research would benefit humans, and perhaps even compensate for human failings. He recently demonstrated a voice-based system that he designed to ask patients about their symptoms and to respond with empathy. When a mother said her child was having diarrhea, the face on the screen said, "Oh no, sorry to hear that."

A physician told him afterward that it was wonderful that the system responded to human emotion. "That's a great idea," Dr. Horvitz said he was told. "I have no time for that."

The Real Threat Posed by Powerful Computers

BY QUENTIN HARDY | JULY 11, 2015

IN OCTOBER, Elon Musk called artificial intelligence "our greatest existential threat," and equated making machines that think with "summoning the demon." In December, Stephen Hawking said "full artificial intelligence could spell the end of the human race." And this year, Bill Gates said he was "concerned about super intelligence," which he appeared to think was just a few decades away.

But if the human race is at peril from killer robots, the problem is probably not artificial intelligence. It is more likely to be artificial stupidity. The difference between those two ideas says much about how we think about computers.

In the kind of artificial intelligence, or A.I., that most people seem to worry about, computers decide people are a bad idea, so they kill them. That is undeniably bad for the human race, but it is a potentially smart move by the computers.

But the real worry, specialists in the field say, is a computer program rapidly overdoing a single task, with no context. A machine that makes paper clips proceeds unfettered, one example goes, and becomes so proficient that overnight we are drowning in paper clips.

In other words, something really dumb happens, at a global scale. As for those "Terminator" robots you tend to see on scary news stories about an A.I. apocalypse, forget it.

"What you should fear is a computer that is competent in one very narrow area, to a bad degree," said Max Tegmark, a professor of physics at the Massachusetts Institute of Technology and the president of the Future of Life Institute, a group dedicated to limiting the risks from A.I.

In late June, when a worker in Germany was killed by an assembly line robot, Mr. Tegmark said, "it was an example of a machine being stupid, not doing something mean but treating a person like a piece of metal."

His institute recently disbursed much of the $10 million that Mr. Musk, the founder of Tesla and SpaceX, gave it to think of ways to prevent autonomous programs from going rogue. Yet even Mr. Musk, along with other luminaries in science and tech, like Mr. Hawking and Mr. Gates, seems to be focused on the wrong potential threat.

There is little sense among practitioners in the field of artificial intelligence that machines are anywhere close to acquiring the kind of consciousness where they could form lethal opinions about their makers.

"These doomsday scenarios confuse the science with remote philosophical problems about the mind and consciousness," Oren Etzioni, chief executive of the Allen Institute for Artificial Intelligence, a nonprofit that explores artificial intelligence, said. "If more people learned how to write software, they'd see how literal-minded these overgrown pencils we call computers actually are."

What accounts for the confusion? One big reason is the way computer scientists work. "The term 'A.I.' came about in the 1950s, when people thought machines that think were around the corner," Mr. Etzioni said. "Now we're stuck with it."

It is still a hallmark of the business. Google's advanced A.I. work is at a company it acquired called DeepMind. A pioneering company in the field was called Thinking Machines. Researchers are pursuing something called Deep Learning, another suggestion that we are birthing intelligence.

Deep Learning relies on a hierarchical reasoning technique called neural networks, suggesting the neurons of a brain. Comparing a node in a neural network to a neuron, though, is at best like comparing a toaster to the space shuttle.

In fairness, the kind of work DeepMind is doing, along with much other work in the burgeoning field of machine learning, does involve spotting patterns, suggesting actions and making predictions. That is akin to the mental stuff people do.

It is among the most exciting fields in tech. There is a pattern-finding race among Amazon, Facebook and Google. Companies including Uber and General Electric are staking much of their future on machine learning.

But machine learning is automation, a better version of what computers have always done. The "learning" is not stored and generalized in the ways that make people smart.

DeepMind made a program that mastered simple video games, but it never took the learning from one game into another. The 22 rungs of a neural net it climbs to figure out what is in a picture do not operate much like human image recognition and are still easily defeated.

Moving out of that stupidity to a broader humanlike capability is called "transfer learning." It is at best in the research phase.

"People in A.I. know that a chess-playing computer still doesn't yearn to capture a queen," said Stuart Russell, a professor of Computer Science at the University of California, Berkeley. He is also on the Future of Life's board and is a recipient of some of Mr. Musk's grant. He seeks mathematical ways to ensure dumb programs don't conflict with our complex human values.

"What the paper clip program lacks is a background value structure," he said. "The misunderstanding is thinking that there is only a threat if there is consciousness."

Elon Musk and Stephen Hawking Among Hundreds to Urge Ban on Military Robots

BY DANIEL VICTOR | JULY 27, 2015

ELON MUSK AND Stephen Hawking, along with hundreds of artificial intelligence researchers and experts, are calling for a worldwide ban on so-called autonomous weapons, warning that they could set off a revolution in weaponry comparable to gunpowder and nuclear arms.

In a letter unveiled as researchers gathered at the International Joint Conference on Artificial Intelligence in Buenos Aires on Monday, the signatories argued that the deployment of robots capable of killing while untethered to human operators is "feasible within years, not decades." If development is not cut off, it is only a matter of time before the weapons end up in the hands of terrorists and warlords, they said.

Unlike drones, which require a person to remotely pilot the craft and make targeting decisions, the autonomous weapons would search for and engage targets on their own. Unlike nuclear weapons, they could be made with raw materials that all significant military powers could afford and obtain, making them easier to mass-produce, the authors argued.

The weapons could reduce military casualties by keeping human soldiers off battlefields, but they could also lower the threshold for going to battle, the letter said. "If any major military power pushes ahead with A.I. weapon development, a global arms race is virtually inevitable, and the endpoint of this technological trajectory is obvious: autonomous weapons will become the Kalashnikovs of tomorrow," it said.

Mr. Musk, the head of SpaceX, has raised warnings about artificial intelligence before, calling it probably humanity's "biggest existential threat." Mr. Hawking, the physicist, has written that while development of artificial intelligence could be the biggest event in human history, "Unfortunately, it might also be the last."

The letter said artificial intelligence "has great potential to benefit humanity in many ways." Proponents have predicted applications in fighting disease, mitigating poverty and carrying out rescues. An association with weaponry, though, could set off a backlash that curtails its advancement, the authors said.

Other notable signatories to the letter included Steve Wozniak, the co-founder of Apple; Noam Chomsky, the linguist and political philosopher; and Demis Hassabis, the chief executive of the artificial intelligence company Google DeepMind.

Mark Zuckerberg, Elon Musk and the Feud Over Killer Robots

BY CADE METZ | JUNE 9, 2018

SAN FRANCISCO — Mark Zuckerberg thought his fellow Silicon Valley billionaire Elon Musk was behaving like an alarmist.

Mr. Musk, the entrepreneur behind SpaceX and the electric-car maker Tesla, had taken it upon himself to warn the world that artificial intelligence was "potentially more dangerous than nukes" in television interviews and on social media.

So, on Nov. 19, 2014, Mr. Zuckerberg, Facebook's chief executive, invited Mr. Musk to dinner at his home in Palo Alto, Calif. Two top researchers from Facebook's new artificial intelligence lab and two other Facebook executives joined them.

As they ate, the Facebook contingent tried to convince Mr. Musk that he was wrong. But he wasn't budging. "I genuinely believe this is dangerous," Mr. Musk told the table, according to one of the dinner's attendees, Yann LeCun, the researcher who led Facebook's A.I. lab.

Mr. Musk's fears of A.I., distilled to their essence, were simple: If we create machines that are smarter than humans, they could turn against us. (See: "The Terminator," "The Matrix," and "2001: A Space Odyssey.") Let's for once, he was saying to the rest of the tech industry, consider the unintended consequences of what we are creating before we unleash it on the world.

Neither Mr. Musk nor Mr. Zuckerberg would talk in detail about the dinner, which has not been reported before, or their long-running A.I. debate.

The creation of "superintelligence" — the name for the supersmart technological breakthrough that takes A.I. to the next level and creates machines that not only perform narrow tasks that typically require human intelligence (like self-driving cars) but can actually outthink humans — still feels like science fiction. But the fight over the future of A.I. has spread across the tech industry.

More than 4,000 Google employees recently signed a petition protesting a $9 million A.I. contract the company had signed with the Pentagon — a deal worth chicken feed to the internet giant, but deeply troubling to many artificial intelligence researchers at the company. Last week, Google executives, trying to head off a worker rebellion, said they wouldn't renew the contract when it expires next year.

Artificial intelligence research has enormous potential and enormous implications, both as an economic engine and a source of military superiority. The Chinese government has said it is willing to spend billions in the coming years to make the country the world's leader in A.I., while the Pentagon is aggressively courting the tech industry for help. A new breed of autonomous weapons can't be far away.

All sorts of deep thinkers have joined the debate, from a gathering of philosophers and scientists held along the central California coast to an annual conference hosted in Palm Springs, Calif., by Amazon's chief executive, Jeff Bezos.

"You can now talk about the risks of A.I. without seeming like you are lost in science fiction," said Allan Dafoe, a director of the governance of A.I. program at the Future of Humanity Institute, a research center at the University of Oxford that explores the risks and opportunities of advanced technology.

And the public roasting of Facebook and other tech companies over the past few months has done plenty to raise the issue of the unintended consequences of the technology created by Silicon Valley.

In April, Mr. Zuckerberg spent two days answering questions from members of Congress about data privacy and Facebook's role in the spread of misinformation before the 2016 election. He faced a similar grilling in Europe last month.

Facebook's recognition that it was slow to understand what was going on has led to a rare moment of self-reflection in an industry that has long believed it is making the world a better place, whether the world likes it or not.

Even such influential figures as the Microsoft founder Bill Gates and the late Stephen Hawking have expressed concern about creating machines that are more intelligent than we are. Even though superintelligence seems decades away, they and others have said, shouldn't we consider the consequences before it's too late?

"The kind of systems we are creating are very powerful," said Bart Selman, a Cornell University computer science professor and former Bell Labs researcher. "And we cannot understand their impact."

THE IMPERFECT MESSENGER

Pacific Grove is a tiny town on the central coast of California. A group of geneticists gathered there, in the winter of 1975 to discuss whether their work — gene editing — would end up harming the world. In January 2017, the A.I. community held a similar discussion in the beachside grove.

The private gathering at the Asilomar Hotel was organized by the Future of Life Institute, a think tank built to discuss the existential risks of A.I. and other technologies.

The heavy hitters of A.I. were in the room — among them Mr. LeCun, the Facebook A.I. lab boss who was at the dinner in Palo Alto, and who had helped develop a neural network, one of the most important tools in artificial intelligence today. Also in attendance was Nick Bostrom, whose 2014 book, "Superintelligence: Paths, Dangers, Strategies" had an outsized — some would argue fear-mongering — effect on the A.I. discussion; Oren Etzioni, a former computer science professor at the University of Washington who had taken over the Allen Institute for Artificial Intelligence in Seattle; and Demis Hassabis, who heads DeepMind, an influential Google-owned A.I. research lab in London.

And so was Mr. Musk, who in 2015 had donated $10 million to the Cambridge, Mass., institute. That same year, he also helped create an independent artificial intelligence lab, OpenAI, with an explicit goal: create superintelligence with safeguards meant to ensure it won't get out of control. It was a message that clearly aligned him with Mr. Bostrom.

On the second day of the retreat, Mr. Musk took part in a nine-person panel dedicated to the superintelligence question. Each panelist was asked if superintelligence was possible. As they passed the microphone down the line, each said "Yes," until the microphone reached Mr. Musk. "No," he said. The small auditorium rippled with knowing laughter. Everyone understood that Mr. Musk thought superintelligence was not only possible, but very dangerous.

Mr. Musk later added: "We are headed toward either superintelligence or civilization ending."

At the end of the panel, Mr. Musk was asked how society can best live alongside superintelligence. What we needed, he said, was a direct connection between our brains and our machines. A few months later, he unveiled a start-up, called Neuralink, backed by $100 million that aimed to create that kind of so-called neural interface by merging computers with human brains.

Warnings about the risks of artificial intelligence have been around for years, of course. But few of those Cassandras have the tech cred of Mr. Musk. Few, if any, have spent as much time and money on it. And perhaps none has had as complicated a history with the technology.

Just a few weeks after Mr. Musk talked about his A.I. concerns at the dinner in Mr. Zuckerberg's house, Mr. Musk phoned Mr. LeCun, asking for the names of top A.I. researchers who could work on his self-driving car project at Tesla. (That autonomous technology was in use at the time of two fatal Tesla car crashes, one in Florida in May 2016 and the other in March of this year.)

During a recent Tesla earnings call, Mr. Musk, who has struggled with questions about his company's financial losses and concerns about the quality of its vehicles, chastised the news media for not focusing on the deaths that autonomous technology could prevent — a remarkable stance from someone who has repeatedly warned the world that A.I. is a danger to humanity.

THE TUSSLE IN PALM SPRINGS

There is a saying in Silicon Valley: We overestimate what can be done in three years and underestimate what can be done in 10.

On Jan. 27, 2016, Google's DeepMind lab unveiled a machine that could beat a professional player at the ancient board game Go. In a match played a few months earlier, the machine, called AlphaGo, had defeated the European champion Fan Hui — five games to none.

Even top A.I. researchers had assumed it would be another decade before a machine could solve the game. Go is complex — there are more possible board positions than atoms in the universe — and the best players win not with sheer calculation, but through intuition. Two weeks before AlphaGo was revealed, Mr. LeCun said the existence of such a machine was unlikely.

A few months later, AlphaGo beat Lee Sedol, the best Go player of the last decade. The machine made moves that baffled human experts but ultimately led to victory.

Many researchers, including the leaders of DeepMind and OpenAI, believe the kind of self-learning technology that underpins AlphaGo provided a path to "superintelligence." And they believe progress in this area will significantly accelerate in the coming years.

OpenAI recently "trained" a system to play a boat racing video game, encouraging it to win as many game points as it could. It proceeded to win those points but did so while spinning in circles, colliding with stone walls and ramming other boats.

It's the kind of unpredictability that raise grave concerns about the rise of A.I., including superintelligence.

But the deep opposition to these concerns was on display in March at an exclusive conference organized by Amazon and Mr. Bezos in Palm Springs.

One evening, Rodney Brooks, a roboticist at the Massachusetts Institute of Technology, debated the potential dangers of A.I. with the neuroscientist, philosopher and podcaster Sam Harris, a prominent voice of caution on the issue. The debate got personal, according to a recording obtained by The Times.

Mr. Harris warned that because the world was in an arms race toward A.I., researchers may not have the time needed to ensure superintelligence is built in a safe way.

"This is something you have made up," Mr. Brooks responded. He implied that Mr. Harris's argument was based on unscientific reasoning. It couldn't be proven right or wrong — a real insult among scientists.

"I would take this personally, if it actually made sense." Mr. Harris said.

A moderator finally ended the tussle and asked for questions from the audience. Mr. Etzioni, the head of the Allen Institute, took the microphone. "I am not going to grandstand," he said. But urged on by Mr. Brooks, he walked onto the stage and laid into Mr. Harris for three minutes, saying that today's A.I. systems are so limited, spending so much time worrying about superintelligence just doesn't make sense.

The people who take Mr. Musk's side are philosophers, social scientists, writers — not the researchers who are working on A.I., he said. Among A.I. scientists, the notion that we should start worrying about superintelligence is "very much a fringe argument."

MR. ZUCKERBERG GOES TO WASHINGTON

Since their dinner three years ago, the debate between Mr. Zuckerberg and Mr. Musk has turned sour. Last summer, in a live Facebook video streamed from his backyard as he and his wife barbecued, Mr. Zuckerberg called Mr. Musk's views on A.I. "pretty irresponsible."

Panicking about A.I. now, so early in its development, could threaten the many benefits that come from things like self-driving cars and A.I. health care, he said.

"With A.I. especially, I'm really optimistic," Mr. Zuckerberg said. "People who are naysayers and kind of try to drum up these doomsday scenarios — I just, I don't understand it."

In other words: You're getting ahead of reality, Elon. Relax.

Mr. Musk responded with a tweet. "I've talked to Mark about this," Mr. Musk wrote. "His understanding of the subject is limited."

In April, Mr. Zuckerberg testified before Congress, explaining how Facebook was going to fix the problems it had helped create.

One way to do it? By leaning on artificial intelligence. But in his testimony, Mr. Zuckerberg acknowledged that scientists haven't exactly figured out how some types of artificial intelligence are learning.

"This is going to be a very central question for how we think about A.I. systems over the next decade and beyond," he said. "Right now, a lot of our A.I. systems make decisions in ways that people don't really understand."

Tech bigwigs and scientists may mock Mr. Musk for his Chicken Little routine on A.I., but they seem to be moving toward his point of view.

Inside Google, a group is exploring flaws in A.I. methods that can fool computer systems into seeing things that are not there. Researchers are warning that A.I. systems that automatically generate realistic images and video will soon make it even harder to trust what we see online. Both DeepMind and OpenAI now operate research groups dedicated to "A.I safety."

Mr. Hassabis, the founder of DeepMind, still thinks Mr. Musk's views are extreme. But he said the same about the views of Mr. Zuckerberg. The threat is not here, he said. Not yet. But Facebook's problems are a warning.

"We need to use the downtime, when things are calm, to prepare for when things get serious in the decades to come," said Mr. Hassabis. "The time we have now is valuable, and we need to make use of it."

Why Silicon Valley Shouldn't Work With the Pentagon

OPINION | BY SCOTT MALCOMSON | APRIL 19, 2018

IS SILICON VALLEY going to war? In 2013, Amazon beat IBM for a contract to host the United States intelligence community's data cloud. Microsoft now markets Azure Government Secret, its cloud-computing service designed specifically for federal and local governments, to the Defense Department and intelligence agencies. And last year, Google signed a contract with the Pentagon for Project Maven, a pilot program to accelerate the military's use of artificial intelligence.

These partnerships might ease anxiety in the Defense Department about China's artificial-intelligence advances and ominous, state-led fusion of civil and military technology development. But a comparable fusion of the United States government and Silicon Valley would be a mistake.

This is not so much because it would compromise Silicon Valley values, as more than 3,000 Google employees argued in a recent letter about Project Maven to the company's chief executive, Sundar Pichai. Rather, it's because the United States' edge in techno-military competition exists in great part because we have a tech sector that is not dominated by the state and its needs.

Narrowing the focus of the United States tech sector to the needs of the military would serve neither party. On the contrary, it would make the nation weaker.

To be sure, defense contracts are hardly new in Silicon Valley, and Google's recent moves might be seen as heralding Silicon Valley's return to its natural home in defense contracting. But that would be to misunderstand both Silicon Valley history and today's technology.

The internet and much of digital computing did indeed emerge from decades of United States defense contracts, beginning as long ago as World War I. Yet the Pentagon itself sloughed off the internet —

not knowing quite what to do with it, and rightly judging it to be insecure — to the National Science Foundation. When the internet became a commercial concern, the National Science Foundation off-loaded it to the Department of Commerce. Government might have given birth to the internet, but it sure didn't raise it.

The emergence of a civilian, entrepreneurial tech culture in the 1970s owed as much intellectually, if not (at first) financially, to the antiwar movement and the 1960s counterculture — hardly friends of the military-industrial complex. Out of this the dominant, highly creative ethos of geek antiauthoritarianism grew. It is hard to believe that closer ties with the military would perpetuate this culture of innovation.

The technology involved in projects like Azure Government Secret and Project Maven is also very different from the data-sharing projects of the 1960s. Those older technologies would not have been created in the absence of government funding. Today's projects, in contrast, are all basically A.I. plays. Very little of this is defense-specific, but all of it is useful for defense and espionage. Unlike, say, weapons development, A.I. research is inherently dual-use. United States tech giants would be pursuing it with or without government contracts. Silicon Valley does not need the Pentagon to initiate these endeavors.

The Pentagon is in a different position. It came around very reluctantly to the idea that it is dependent on private industry for the defense of the country and the projection of American power. But come around it has, in no small part thanks to China.

China's state interest in A.I. was initially economic, but military uses were never far behind. As Elsa B. Kania, a researcher at the Center for a New American Security, explained in an influential report, "A.I. is a high-level priority within China's national agenda for military-civil fusion," a strategy that should allow the Chinese armed forces to benefit from private-sector advances in A.I.

The United States military seems to have been spooked. In a 2017 memo, the deputy secretary of defense, Robert O. Work, wrote that while the Defense Department had made "tentative steps" in A.I., "we need to do much more, and move much faster." The memo announced the formation of Project Maven to do just that. This month, Gen. Stephen Wilson, the vice chief of staff for the Air Force, said that China is taking a "whole of nation" approach to A.I. and the United States should, too.

Yet we shouldn't forget that civil-military antagonism and the deep American tradition of distrusting the state have been crucial to the United States' ability to innovate. There are good reasons why defense-tech giants of the 1960s, '70s and '80s like Raytheon and Grumman missed out on such major tech advances as Web protocols, the smartphone, personal computers and various types of encryption — all of which would eventually have great military significance. The biggest reason was that none of these advances were directed at waging war; indeed, many aimed at transcending the power of the state.

After the Cold War, the Soviet Union's extraordinary technological capacity dissipated in large part because it had been so reactive: The Soviets had let their adversary determine the pace and scope of their own innovation. The United States should not make that mistake.

SCOTT MALCOMSON (@smalcomson) is the director of special projects at Strategic Insight Group, a former State Department official and the author of "Splinternet: How Geopolitics and Commerce Are Fragmenting the World Wide Web."

Google Promises Its A.I. Will Not Be Used for Weapons

BY DAISUKE WAKABAYASHI AND CADE METZ | JUNE 7, 2018

SAN FRANCISCO — Google, reeling from an employee protest over the use of artificial intelligence for military purposes, said Thursday that it would not use A.I. for weapons or for surveillance that violates human rights. But it will continue to work with governments and the military.

The new rules were part of a set of principles Google unveiled relating to the use of artificial intelligence. In a company blog post, Sundar Pichai, the chief executive, laid out seven objectives for its A.I. technology, including "avoid creating or reinforcing unfair bias" and "be socially beneficial."

Google also detailed applications of the technology that the company will not pursue, including A.I. for "weapons or other technologies whose principal purpose or implementation is to cause or directly facilitate injury to people" and "technologies that gather or use information for surveillance violating internationally accepted norms of human rights."

But Google said it would continue to work with governments and military using A.I. in areas including cybersecurity, training and military recruitment.

"We recognize that such powerful technology raises equally powerful questions about its use. How A.I. is developed and used will have a significant impact on society for many years to come," Mr. Pichai wrote.

Concern over the potential uses of artificial intelligence bubbled over at Google when the company secured a contract to work on the Pentagon's Project Maven program, which uses A.I. to interpret video images and could be used to improve the targeting of drone strikes.

More than 4,000 Google employees signed a petition protesting the contract, and a handful of employees resigned. In response, Google said it would not seek to renew the Maven contract when it expired next year and pledged to draft a set of guidelines for appropriates uses of A.I.

Mr. Pichai did not address the Maven program or the pressure from employees. It's not clear whether these guidelines would have precluded Google from pursuing the Maven contract, since the company has insisted repeatedly that its work for the Pentagon was not for "offensive purposes."

Google has bet its future on artificial intelligence, and company executives believe the technology could have an impact comparable to the development of the internet.

Google promotes the benefits of artificial intelligence for tasks like early diagnosis of diseases and the reduction of spam in email. But it has also experienced some of the perils associated with A.I., including YouTube recommendations pushing users to extremist videos or Google Photos image-recognition software categorizing black people as gorillas.

While most of Google's A.I. guidelines are unsurprising for a company that prides itself on altruistic goals, it also included a noteworthy rule about how its technology could be shared outside the company.

"We will reserve the right to prevent or stop uses of our technology if we become aware of uses that are inconsistent with these principles," the company said.

Like most of the top corporate A.I. labs, which are laden with former and current academics, Google openly publishes much of its A.I. research. That means others can recreate and reuse many of its methods and ideas. But Google is joining other labs in saying it may hold back certain research if it believes others will misuse it.

DeepMind, a top A.I. lab owned by Google's parent company, Alphabet, is considering whether it should refrain from publishing certain research because it may be dangerous. OpenAI, a lab founded by the Tesla chief executive Elon Musk and others, recently released a new charter indicating it could do much the same — even though it was founded on the principle that it would openly share all its research.

As Artificial Intelligence Evolves, So Does Its Criminal Potential

BY JOHN MARKOFF | OCT. 23, 2016

IMAGINE RECEIVING A phone call from your aging mother seeking your help because she has forgotten her banking password.

Except it's not your mother. The voice on the other end of the phone call just sounds deceptively like her.

It is actually a computer-synthesized voice, a tour-de-force of artificial intelligence technology that has been crafted to make it possible for someone to masquerade via the telephone.

Such a situation is still science fiction — but just barely. It is also the future of crime.

The software components necessary to make such masking technology widely accessible are advancing rapidly. Recently, for example, DeepMind, the Alphabet subsidiary known for a program that has bested some of the top human players in the board game Go, announced that it had designed a program that "mimics any human voice and which sounds more natural than the best existing text-to-speech systems, reducing the gap with human performance by over 50 percent."

The irony, of course, is that this year the computer security industry, with $75 billion in annual revenue, has started to talk about how machine learning and pattern recognition techniques will improve the woeful state of computer security.

But there is a downside.

"The thing people don't get is that cybercrime is becoming automated and it is scaling exponentially," said Marc Goodman, a law enforcement agency adviser and the author of "Future Crimes." He added, "This is not about Matthew Broderick hacking from his basement," a reference to the 1983 movie "War Games."

The alarm about malevolent use of advanced artificial intelligence technologies was sounded earlier this year by James R. Clapper, the director of National Intelligence. In his annual review of security, Mr. Clapper underscored the point that while A.I. systems would make some things easier, they would also expand the vulnerabilities of the online world.

The growing sophistication of computer criminals can be seen in the evolution of attack tools like the widely used malicious program known as Blackshades, according to Mr. Goodman. The author of the program, a Swedish national, was convicted last year in the United States.

The system, which was sold widely in the computer underground, functioned as a "criminal franchise in a box," Mr. Goodman said. It allowed users without technical skills to deploy computer ransomware or perform video or audio eavesdropping with a mouse click.

The next generation of these tools will add machine learning capabilities that have been pioneered by artificial intelligence researchers to improve the quality of machine vision, speech understanding, speech synthesis and natural language understanding. Some computer security researchers believe that digital criminals have been experimenting with the use of A.I. technologies for more than half a decade.

That can be seen in efforts to subvert the internet's omnipresent Captcha — Completely Automated Public Turing test to tell Computers and Humans Apart — the challenge-and-response puzzle invented in 2003 by Carnegie Mellon University researchers to block automated programs from stealing online accounts.

Both "white hat" artificial intelligence researchers and "black hat" criminals have been deploying machine vision software to subvert Captchas for more than half a decade, said Stefan Savage, a computer security researcher at the University of California, San Diego.

"If you don't change your Captcha for two years, you will be owned by some machine vision algorithm," he said.

Surprisingly, one thing that has slowed the development of malicious A.I. has been the ready availability of either low-cost or free human labor. For example, some cybercriminals have farmed out Captcha-breaking schemes to electronic sweatshops where humans are used to decode the puzzles for a tiny fee.

Even more inventive computer crooks have used online pornography as a reward for human web surfers who break the Captcha, Mr. Goodman said. Free labor is a commodity that A.I. software won't be able to compete with any time soon.

So what's next?

Criminals, for starters, can piggyback on new tech developments. Voice-recognition technology like Apple's Siri and Microsoft's Cortana are now used extensively to interact with computers. And Amazon's Echo voice-controlled speaker and Facebook's Messenger chatbot platform are rapidly becoming conduits for online commerce and customer support. As is often the case, whenever a communication advancement like voice recognition starts to go mainstream, criminals looking to take advantage of it aren't far behind.

"I would argue that companies that offer customer support via chatbots are unwittingly making themselves liable to social engineering," said Brian Krebs, an investigative reporter who publishes at krebsonsecurity.com.

Social engineering, which refers to the practice of manipulating people into performing actions or divulging information, is widely seen as the weakest link in the computer security chain. Cybercriminals already exploit the best qualities in humans — trust and willingness to help others — to steal and spy. The ability to create artificial intelligence avatars that can fool people online will only make the problem worse.

This can already be seen in efforts by state governments and political campaigns who are using chatbot technology widely for political propaganda.

Researchers have coined the term "computational propaganda" to describe the explosion of deceptive social media campaigns on services like Facebook and Twitter.

In a recent research paper, Philip N. Howard, a sociologist at the Oxford Internet Institute, and Bence Kollanyi, a researcher at Corvinus University of Budapest, described how political chatbots had a "small but strategic role" in shaping the online conversation during the run-up to the "Brexit" referendum.

It is only a matter of time before such software is put to criminal use.

"There's a lot of cleverness in designing social engineering attacks, but as far as I know, nobody has yet started using machine learning to find the highest quality suckers," said Mark Seiden, an independent computer security specialist. He paused and added, "I should have replied: 'I'm sorry, Dave, I can't answer that question right now.' "

'Intelligent' Policing and My Innocent Children

OPINION | BY BÄRÍ A. WILLIAMS | DEC. 2, 2017

OAKLAND, CALIF. — Last month I spoke at a gathering of African-American technology professionals. I'm a transactional lawyer at a tech company and my husband is an engineer, so the industry is at the center of our lives. We have careers that allow us to help create products and tools our grandparents would never have thought were possible and to provide the kind of life for our family that they couldn't have imagined. And it's important to us to ensure that other people of color have a chance to contribute to the field and reap its benefits. With all those things on my mind, I left the conference energized and inspired by the ways in which tech is changing the world and the possibilities it holds for our community.

At the same time, I'm terrified for what these advances mean for my two young children. The same technology that's the source of so much excitement in my career is being used in law enforcement in ways that could mean that in the coming years, my son, who is 7 now, is more likely to be profiled or arrested — or worse — for no reason other than his race and where we live.

Of course I'm not alone in feeling that technology is both a gift and a curse. This tension exists for anyone who enjoys the real-time conversations on Twitter but loathes the trolls, loves Facebook but abhors fake news, or depends on the convenience Alexa offers but frets about violations of privacy.

Yet in my life, because of the way artificial intelligence and machine learning are being increasingly used by law enforcement — the technology is seemingly growing up alongside my kids — it's especially acute.

Unjust racial profiling and resulting racial disparities in the criminal justice system certainly don't depend on artificial intelligence. But when you add it — as many law enforcement agencies across the country, including those in major cities like Miami, Los Angeles,

Philadelphia, Atlanta and New York, have over the past couple of years — things get even scarier for black families.

This is especially frightening when combined with the fact that the current administration has already begun to reverse Obama-era criminal justice reform policies that were meant to make the system more just.

A.I. works by taking large volumes of information and distilling it down to simple concepts, categories and rules and then predicting future responses and outcomes. This is a function of the beliefs, assumptions and capabilities of the people who do the coding. A.I. learns by repetition and association, and all of that is based on the information we — humans who hold all the racial and often, specifically, anti-black biases of our society — feed it.

Just think of how Google's facial recognition programs labeled black people in photos "gorillas." Or how Microsoft's Tay, a bot designed to engage in Twitter conversations, devolved into a racial-epithet-tweeting machine within 24 hours.

These downsides of A.I. are no secret. Despite this, state and local law enforcement agencies have begun to use predictive policing applications fueled by A.I. like HunchLab, which combines historical crime data, moon phases, location, census data and even professional sports team schedules to predict when and where crime will occur and even who's likely to commit or be a victim of certain crimes.

The problem with historical crime data is that it's based upon policing practices that already disproportionately home in on blacks, Latinos, and those who live in low-income areas.

If the police have discriminated in the past, predictive technology reinforces and perpetuates the problem, sending more officers after people who we know are already targeted and unfairly treated, given recent evidence like the Justice Department's reports on Ferguson, Mo., and Baltimore, and the findings of the San Francisco Blue Ribbon Panel on Transparency Accountability and Fairness in Law Enforcement.

It's no wonder criminologists have raised red flags about the self-fulfilling nature of using historical crime data.

This hits close to home. An October 2016 study by the Human Rights Data Analysis Group concluded that if the Oakland Police Department used its 2010 record of drug-crimes information as the basis of an algorithm to guide policing, the department "would have dispatched officers almost exclusively to lower-income, minority neighborhoods," despite the fact that public-health-based estimates suggest that drug use is much more widespread, taking place in many other parts of the city where my family and I live.

Those "lower-income, minority neighborhoods" contain the barbershop where I take my son for his monthly haircut and our favorite hoagie shop. Would I let him run ahead of me if I knew that simply setting foot on those sidewalks would make him more likely to be seen as a criminal in the eyes of the law?

The risks are even more acute (and unavoidable) for those who can afford to live only in the neighborhoods that A.I. would most likely lead officers to focus on.

There's yet another opportunity for racial bias to infuse the process when risk-assessment algorithms created by A.I. and machine learning are used to help to sentence criminals, as they already are in courts around the country.

Without a commitment to ensure that the data being used to fuel A.I. doesn't replicate historical racism, biases will be built into the foundation of many "intelligent" systems shaping how we live. It's not that I want this technology to be rejected. There are ways to make A.I. work. But before it is used in law enforcement, it must be thoroughly tested and proven not to disproportionately harm communities of color.

Until then my excitement about advances in tech will always be cautious. Innovation is at the core of the careers that allow me and my husband to provide a good life for our family. The same innovation, if not used properly, could take it all away.

BÄRÍ A. WILLIAMS is a legal and operations executive in the tech industry and start-up adviser.

When the Robot Doesn't See Dark Skin

OPINION | BY JOY BUOLAMWINI | JUNE 21, 2018

WHEN I WAS a college student using A.I.-powered facial detection software for a coding project, the robot I programmed couldn't detect my dark-skinned face. I had to borrow my white roommate's face to finish the assignment. Later, working on another project as a graduate student at the M.I.T. Media Lab, I resorted to wearing a white mask to have my presence recognized.

My experience is a reminder that artificial intelligence, often heralded for its potential to change the world, can actually reinforce bias and exclusion, even when it's used in the most well-intended ways.

A.I. systems are shaped by the priorities and prejudices — conscious and unconscious — of the people who design them, a phenomenon that I refer to as "the coded gaze." Research has shown that automated systems that are used to inform decisions about sentencing produce results that are biased against black people and that those used for selecting the targets of online advertising can discriminate based on race and gender.

Specifically, when it comes to algorithmic bias in facial analysis technology — my area of research and one focus of my work with the Algorithmic Justice League — Google's photo application labeling black people in images as "gorillas" and facial analysis software that works well for white men but less so for everyone else are infamous examples. As disturbing as they are, they do not fully capture the risks of this technology that is increasingly being used in law enforcement, border control, school surveillance and hiring.

The products of a company called HireVue, which are used by over 600 companies including Nike, Unilever and even Atlanta Public Schools, allow employers to interview job applicants on camera, using A.I. to rate videos of each candidate according to verbal and nonverbal cues. The company's aim is to reduce bias in hiring.

But there's a catch: The system's ratings, according to a Business Insider reporter who tested the software and discussed the results with HireVue's chief technology officer, reflect the previous preferences of hiring managers. So if more white males with generally homogeneous mannerisms have been hired in the past, it's possible that algorithms will be trained to favorably rate predominantly fair-skinned, male candidates while penalizing women and people of color who do not exhibit the same verbal and nonverbal cues.

It's repeatedly been proven that apart from technology, people tend to make hiring decisions favoring white and male candidates, all other things being equal. With this in mind, the instinct to hand the rating of potential employees over to technology is understandable. But how do we know a qualified candidate whose verbal and nonverbal cues tied to age, gender, sexual orientation or race depart from those of the high performers used to train the algorithm will not be scored lower than a similar candidate who more closely resembles the in-group? We won't know if we do not repeatedly test the technology and its application.

The tests that have been done on facial analysis technology raise concerns. In collaboration with the computer vision expert Timnit Gebru, I investigated the accuracy of facial analysis technology from IBM, Microsoft and Face++. On the simple task of guessing the gender of a face, all companies' technology performed better on male faces than on female faces and especially struggled on the faces of dark-skinned African women. In the worst case, the technology was 34 percent less accurate for those women than it was for white men.

Given how susceptible facial analysis technology seems to recreating gender and racial bias, companies using HireVue, if they hope to increase fairness, should check their systems to make sure it is not amplifying the biases that informed previous hiring decisions. It's possible companies using HireVue could someday face lawsuits charging that the program had a negative disparate impact on women and minority applicants, a violation of Title VII of the Civil Rights Act.

The risks of biased facial analysis technology extend beyond hiring. According to the Center on Privacy and Technology at Georgetown Law, the faces of half of all adults in the United States — over 117 million people — are currently in face recognition database networks that can be searched by police departments without warrant. These searches are often reliant on facial recognition technology that hasn't been tested for accuracy on different groups of people. This matters because misidentification can subject innocent people to police scrutiny or erroneous criminal charges.

In the case of South Wales, where Big Brother Watch reports that between May 2017 and March 2018 the faces of over 2,400 misidentified innocent people were stored by the police department without their consent, the department reported a false-positive facial identification rate of 91 percent. But it's important to remember that even if false-positive match rates improve, unfair use of facial recognition technology cannot be fixed with a software patch. Even accurate facial recognition can be used in disturbing ways. The Baltimore police department used face recognition technology to identify and arrest people who attended the 2015 protests against police misconduct that followed Freddie Gray's death in Baltimore.

We need to challenge the growing use of this technology, and there has been some progress on this front. The A.C.L.U. is calling on Amazon to stop selling facial analysis technology to law enforcement and is contesting the use of in-car facial recognition for the Vehicle Face System being tested at the United States-Mexico border. Though lawmakers in Texas, Illinois and California have made legislative efforts to regulate facial recognition technology, there are no federal laws. Yet, there is a blueprint. A 2016 report from Georgetown Law School proposed model federal legislation. Policymakers should embrace it.

We can also learn from international models. Unlike the United States, Canada has a federal statute governing the use of biometric data in the private sector. Companies like Facebook and Amazon must obtain informed consent to collect citizens' unique face information. In the European Union, Article 9 of the General Data Protection Regulation requires express affirmative consent for collection of biometrics from E.U. citizens.

Everyday people should support lawmakers, activists and public-interest technologists in demanding transparency, equity and accountability in the use of artificial intelligence that governs our lives. Facial recognition is increasingly penetrating our lives, but there is still time to prevent it from worsening social inequalities. To do that, we must face the coded gaze.

JOY BUOLAMWINI (@jovialjoy) is the founder of the Algorithmic Justice League and a graduate researcher at the M.I.T. Media Lab.

Here Come the Fake Videos, Too

BY KEVIN ROOSE | MARCH 4, 2018

Artificial intelligence video tools make it relatively easy to put one person's face on another person's body with few traces of manipulation. I tried it on myself. What could go wrong?

THE SCENE OPENED on a room with a red sofa, a potted plant and the kind of bland modern art you'd see on a therapist's wall.

In the room was Michelle Obama, or someone who looked exactly like her. Wearing a low-cut top with a black bra visible underneath, she writhed lustily for the camera and flashed her unmistakable smile.

Then, the former first lady's doppelgänger began to strip.

The video, which appeared on the online forum Reddit, was what's known as a "deepfake" — an ultrarealistic fake video made with artificial intelligence software. It was created using a program called FakeApp, which superimposed Mrs. Obama's face onto the body of a pornographic film actress. The hybrid was uncanny — if you didn't know better, you might have thought it was really her.

Until recently, realistic computer-generated video was a laborious pursuit available only to big-budget Hollywood productions or cutting-edge researchers. Social media apps like Snapchat include some rudimentary face-morphing technology.

But in recent months, a community of hobbyists has begun experimenting with more powerful tools, including FakeApp — a program that was built by an anonymous developer using open-source software written by Google. FakeApp makes it free and relatively easy to create realistic face swaps and leave few traces of manipulation. Since a version of the app appeared on Reddit in January, it has been downloaded more than 120,000 times, according to its creator.

Deepfakes are one of the newest forms of digital media manipulation, and one of the most obviously mischief-prone. It's not hard to imagine this technology's being used to smear politicians, create counterfeit revenge porn or frame people for crimes. Lawmakers have already begun to worry about how deepfakes could be used for political sabotage and propaganda.

Even on morally lax sites like Reddit, deepfakes have raised eyebrows. Recently, FakeApp set off a panic after Motherboard, the technology site, reported that people were using it to create pornographic deepfakes of celebrities. Pornhub, Twitter and other sites quickly banned the videos, and Reddit closed a handful of deepfake groups, including one with nearly 100,000 members.

Before the Reddit deepfake groups were closed, they hosted a mixture of users trading video-editing tips and showing off their latest forgeries. A post titled "3D face reconstruction for additional angles" sat next to videos with titles like "(Not) Olivia Wilde playing with herself."

Some users on Reddit defended deepfakes and blamed the media for overhyping their potential for harm. Others moved their videos to alternative platforms, rightly anticipating that Reddit would crack down under its rules against nonconsensual pornography. And a few expressed moral qualms about putting the technology into the world.

Then, they kept making more.

The deepfake creator community is now in the internet's shadows. But while out in the open, it gave an unsettling peek into the future.

"This is turning into an episode of Black Mirror," wrote one Reddit user. The post raised the ontological questions at the heart of the deepfake debate: Does a naked image of Person A become a naked image of Person B if Person B's face is superimposed in a seamless and untraceable way? In a broader sense, on the internet, what is the difference between representation and reality?

The user then signed off with a shrug: "Godspeed rebels."

MAKING DEEPFAKES

After lurking for several weeks in Reddit's deepfake community, I decided to see how easy it was to create a (safe for work, nonpornographic) deepfake using my own face.

I started by downloading FakeApp and enlisting two technical experts to help me. The first was Mark McKeague, a colleague in The New York Times's research and development department. The second was a deepfake creator I found through Reddit, who goes by the nickname Derpfakes.

Because of the controversial nature of deepfakes, Derpfakes would not give his or her real name. Derpfakes started posting deepfake videos on YouTube a few weeks ago, specializing in humorous offerings like Nicolas Cage playing Superman. The account has also posted some how-to videos on deepfake creation.

What I learned is that making a deepfake isn't simple. But it's not rocket science, either.

The first step is to find, or rent, a moderately powerful computer. FakeApp uses a suite of machine learning tools called TensorFlow, which was developed by Google's A.I. division and released to the public in 2015. The software teaches itself to perform image-recognition tasks through trial and error. The more processing power on hand, the faster it works.

To get more speed, Mark and I used a remote server rented through Google Cloud Platform. It provided enough processing power to cut the time frame down to hours, rather than the days or weeks it might take on my laptop.

Once Mark set up the remote server and loaded FakeApp on it, we were on to the next step: data collection.

Picking the right source data is crucial. Short video clips are easier to manipulate than long clips, and scenes shot at a single angle produce better results than scenes with multiple angles. Genetics also help. The more the faces resemble each other, the better.

I'm a brown-haired white man with a short beard, so Mark and I decided to try several other brown-haired, stubbled white guys. We started with Ryan Gosling. (Aim high, right?) I also sent Derpfakes, my outsourced Reddit expert, several video options to choose from.

Next, we took several hundred photos of my face, and gathered images of Mr. Gosling's face using a clip from a recent TV appearance. FakeApp uses these images to train the deep learning model and teach it to emulate our facial expressions.

To get the broadest photo set possible, I twisted my head at different angles, making as many different faces as I could.

Mark then used a program to crop those images down, isolating just our faces, and manually deleted any blurred or badly cropped photos. He then fed the frames into FakeApp. In all, we used 417 photos of me, and 1,113 of Mr. Gosling.

When the images were ready, Mark pressed "start" on FakeApp, and the training began. His computer screen filled with images of my face and Mr. Gosling's face, as the program tried to identify patterns and similarities.

About eight hours later, after our model had been sufficiently trained, Mark used FakeApp to finish putting my face on Mr. Gosling's body. The video was blurry and bizarre, and Mr. Gosling's face occasionally flickered into view. Only the legally blind would mistake the person in the video for me.

We did better with a clip of Chris Pratt, the scruffy star of "Jurassic World," whose face shape is a little more similar to mine. For this test, Mark used a bigger data set — 1,861 photos of me, 1,023 of him — and let the model run overnight.

A few days later, Derpfakes, who had also been training a model, sent me a finished deepfake made using the footage I had sent and a video of the actor Jake Gyllenhaal. This one was much more lifelike, a true hybrid that mixed my facial features with his hair, beard and body.

Derpfakes repeated the process with videos of Jimmy Kimmel and Liev Schreiber, both of which turned out well. As an experienced deepfake creator, Derpfakes had a more intuitive sense of which source videos would produce a clean result, and more experience with the subtle blending and tweaking that takes place at the end of the deepfake process.

In all, our deepfake experiment took three days and cost $85.96 in Google Cloud Platform credits. That seemed like a small price to pay for stardom.

WHAT THE APP'S CREATOR SAYS

After the experiment, I reached out to the anonymous creator of FakeApp through an email address on its website. I wanted to know how it felt to create a cutting-edge A.I. tool, only to have it gleefully co-opted by ethically challenged pornographers.

A man wrote back, identifying himself as a software developer in Maryland. Like Derpfakes, the man would not give me his full name, and instead went by his first initial, N. He said he had created FakeApp as a creative experiment and was chagrined to see Reddit's deepfake community use it for ill.

"I joined the community based around these algorithms when it was very small (less than 500 people)," he wrote, "and as soon as I saw the results I knew this was brilliant tech that should be accessible to anyone who wants to play around with it. I figured I'd take a shot at putting together an easy-to-use package to accomplish that."

N. said he didn't support the use of FakeApp to create nonconsensual pornography or other abusive content. And he said he agreed with Reddit's decision to ban explicit deepfakes. But he defended the product.

"I've given it a lot of thought," he said, "and ultimately I've decided I don't think it's right to condemn the technology itself — which can of course be used for many purposes, good and bad."

FakeApp is somewhat finicky and hard to use, but it's easy to imagine it improving quickly. N. said that in the future, FakeApp could be used by all kinds of people to bring high-budget special effects to their personal projects.

Deep learning algorithms, he added, were going to be important in the future, not only as stand-alone apps but as powerful components of many tech products.

"It's precisely the things that make them so powerful and useful that make them so scary," he said. "There's really no limit to what you can apply it to with a little imagination."

'NEXT FORM OF COMMUNICATION'

On the day of the school shooting last month in Parkland, Fla., a screenshot of a BuzzFeed News article, "Why We Need to Take Away White People's Guns Now More Than Ever," written by a reporter named Richie Horowitz, began making the rounds on social media.

The whole thing was fake. No BuzzFeed employee named Richie Horowitz exists, and no article with that title was ever published on the site. But the doctored image pulsed through right-wing outrage channels and was boosted by activists on Twitter. It wasn't an A.I.-generated deepfake, or even a particularly sophisticated Photoshop job, but it did the trick.

Online misinformation, no matter how sleekly produced, spreads through a familiar process once it enters our social distribution channels. The hoax gets 50,000 shares, and the debunking an hour later gets 200. The carnival barker gets an algorithmic boost on services like Facebook and YouTube, while the expert screams into the void.

There's no reason to believe that deepfake videos will operate any differently. People will share them when they're ideologically convenient and dismiss them when they're not. The dupes who fall for satirical stories from The Onion will be fooled by deepfakes, and the scrupulous people who care about the truth will find ways to detect and debunk them.

"There's no choice," said Hao Li, an assistant professor of computer science at the University of Southern California. Mr. Li, who is also the founder of Pinscreen, a company that uses artificial intelligence to create lifelike 3-D avatars, said the weaponization of A.I. was inevitable and would require a sudden shift in public awareness.

"I see this as the next form of communication," he said. "I worry that people will use it to blackmail others, or do bad things. You have to educate people that this is possible."

So, O.K. Here I am, telling you this: An A.I. program powerful enough to turn Michelle Obama into a pornography star, or transform a schlubby newspaper columnist into Jake Gyllenhaal, is in our midst. Manipulated video will soon become far more commonplace.

And there's probably nothing we can do except try to bat the fakes down as they happen, pressure social media companies to fight misinformation aggressively, and trust our eyes a little less every day.

Godspeed, rebels.

Inside China's Dystopian Dreams: A.I., Shame and Lots of Cameras

BY PAUL MOZUR | JULY 8, 2018

ZHENGZHOU, CHINA — In the Chinese city of Zhengzhou, a police officer wearing facial recognition glasses spotted a heroin smuggler at a train station.

In Qingdao, a city famous for its German colonial heritage, cameras powered by artificial intelligence helped the police snatch two dozen criminal suspects in the midst of a big annual beer festival.

In Wuhu, a fugitive murder suspect was identified by a camera as he bought food from a street vendor.

With millions of cameras and billions of lines of code, China is building a high-tech authoritarian future. Beijing is embracing technologies like facial recognition and artificial intelligence to identify and track 1.4 billion people. It wants to assemble a vast and unprecedented national surveillance system, with crucial help from its thriving technology industry.

"In the past, it was all about instinct," said Shan Jun, the deputy chief of the police at the railway station in Zhengzhou, where the heroin smuggler was caught. "If you missed something, you missed it."

China is reversing the commonly held vision of technology as a great democratizer, bringing people more freedom and connecting them to the world. In China, it has brought control.

In some cities, cameras scan train stations for China's most wanted. Billboard-size displays show the faces of jaywalkers and list the names of people who don't pay their debts. Facial recognition scanners guard the entrances to housing complexes. Already, China has an estimated 200 million surveillance cameras — four times as many as the United States.

Such efforts supplement other systems that track internet use and communications, hotel stays, train and plane trips and even car travel in some places.

GILLES SABRIÉ FOR THE NEW YORK TIMES

A video showing facial recognition software in use at the headquarters of the artificial intelligence company Megvii in Beijing.

Even so, China's ambitions outstrip its abilities. Technology in place at one train station or crosswalk may be lacking in another city, or even the next block over. Bureaucratic inefficiencies prevent the creation of a nationwide network.

For the Communist Party, that may not matter. Far from hiding their efforts, Chinese authorities regularly state, and overstate, their capabilities. In China, even the perception of surveillance can keep the public in line.

Some places are further along than others. Invasive mass-surveillance software has been set up in the west to track members of the Uighur Muslim minority and map their relations with friends and family, according to software viewed by The New York Times.

"This is potentially a totally new way for the government to manage the economy and society," said Martin Chorzempa, a fellow at the Peterson Institute for International Economics.

"The goal is algorithmic governance," he added.

THE SHAME GAME

The intersection south of Changhong Bridge in the city of Xiangyang used to be a nightmare. Cars drove fast and jaywalkers darted into the street.

Then last summer, the police put up cameras linked to facial recognition technology and a big, outdoor screen. Photos of lawbreakers were displayed alongside their names and government I.D. numbers. People were initially excited to see their faces on the board, said Guan Yue, a spokeswoman, until propaganda outlets told them it was punishment.

"If you are captured by the system and you don't see it, your neighbors or colleagues will, and they will gossip about it," she said. "That's too embarrassing for people to take."

China's new surveillance is based on an old idea: Only strong authority can bring order to a turbulent country. Mao Zedong took that philosophy to devastating ends, as his top-down rule brought famine and then the Cultural Revolution.

His successors also craved order but feared the consequences of totalitarian rule. They formed a new understanding with the Chinese people. In exchange for political impotence, they would be mostly left alone and allowed to get rich.

It worked. Censorship and police powers remained strong, but China's people still found more freedom. That new attitude helped usher in decades of breakneck economic growth.

Today, that unwritten agreement is breaking down.

China's economy isn't growing at the same pace. It suffers from a severe wealth gap. After four decades of fatter paychecks and better living, its people have higher expectations.

Xi Jinping, China's top leader, has moved to solidify his power. Changes to Chinese law mean he could rule longer than any leader since Mao. And he has undertaken a broad corruption crackdown that could make him plenty of enemies.

For support, he has turned to the Mao-era beliefs in the importance of a cult of personality and the role of the Communist Party in everyday life. Technology gives him the power to make it happen.

"Reform and opening has already failed, but no one dares to say it," said Chinese historian Zhang Lifan, citing China's four-decade post-Mao policy. "The current system has created severe social and economic segregation. So now the rulers use the taxpayers' money to monitor the taxpayers."

Mr. Xi has launched a major upgrade of the Chinese surveillance state. China has become the world's biggest market for security and surveillance technology, with analysts estimating the country will have almost 300 million cameras installed by 2020. Chinese buyers will snap up more than three-quarters of all servers designed to scan video footage for faces, predicts IHS Markit, a research firm. China's police will spend an additional $30 billion in the coming years on techno-enabled snooping, according to one expert quoted in state media.

Government contracts are fueling research and development into technologies that track faces, clothing and even a person's gait. Experimental gadgets, like facial-recognition glasses, have begun to appear.

Judging public Chinese reaction can be difficult in a country where the news media is controlled by the government. Still, so far the average Chinese citizen appears to show little concern. Erratic enforcement of laws against everything from speeding to assault means the long arm of China's authoritarian government can feel remote from everyday life. As a result, many cheer on new attempts at law and order.

"It's one of the biggest intersections in the city," said Wang Fukang, a college student who volunteered as a guard at the crosswalk in Xiangyang. "It's important that it stays safe and orderly."

THE SURVEILLANCE START-UP

Start-ups often make a point of insisting their employees use their technology. In Shanghai, a company called Yitu has taken that to the extreme.

The halls of its offices are dotted with cameras, looking for faces. From desk to break room to exit, employees' paths are traced on a television screen with blue dotted lines. The monitor shows their comings and goings, all day, everyday.

In China, snooping is becoming big business. As the country spends heavily on surveillance, a new generation of start-ups have risen to meet the demand.

Chinese companies are developing globally competitive applications like image and voice recognition. Yitu took first place in a 2017 open contest for facial recognition algorithms held by the United States government's Office of the Director of National Intelligence. A number of other Chinese companies also scored well.

A technology boom in China is helping the government's surveillance ambitions. In sheer scale and investment, China already rivals Silicon Valley. Between the government and eager investors, surveillance start-ups have access to plenty of money and other resources.

In May, the upstart A.I. company SenseTime raised $620 million, giving it a valuation of about $4.5 billion. Yitu raised $200 million last month. Another rival, Megvii, raised $460 million from investors that included a state-backed fund created by China's top leadership.

At a conference in May at an upscale hotel in Beijing, China's security-industrial complex offered its vision of the future. Companies big and small showed off facial-recognition security gates and systems that track cars around cities to local government officials, tech executives and investors.

Private companies see big potential in China's surveillance build-out. China's public security market was valued at more than $80 billion last year but could be worth even more as the country builds its capabilities, said Shen Xinyang, a former Google data scientist who is now chief technology officer of Eyecool, a start-up.

"Artificial intelligence for public security is actually still a very insignificant portion of the whole market," he said, pointing out that most equipment currently in use was "nonintelligent."

Many of these businesses are already providing data to the government.

Mr. Shen told the group that his company had surveillance systems at more than 20 airports and train stations, which had helped catch 1,000 criminals. Eyecool, he said, is also handing over two million facial images each day to a burgeoning big-data police system called Skynet.

At a building complex in Xiangyang, a facial-recognition system set up to let residents quickly through security gates adds to the police's collection of photos of local residents, according to local Chinese Communist Party officials.

Wen Yangli, an executive at Number 1 Community, which makes the product, said the company is at work on other applications. One would detect when crowds of people are clashing. Another would allow police to use virtual maps of buildings to find out who lives where.

China's surveillance companies are also looking to test the appetite for high-tech surveillance abroad. Yitu says it has been expanding overseas, with plans to increase business in regions like Southeast Asia and the Middle East.

At home, China is preparing its people for next-level surveillance technology. A recent state-media propaganda film called "Amazing China" showed off a similar virtual map that provided police with records of utility use, saying it could be used for predictive policing.

"If there are anomalies, the system sends an alert," a narrator says, as Chinese police officers pay a visit to an apartment with a record of erratic utility use. The film then quotes one of the officers: "No matter which corner you escape to, we'll bring you to justice."

ENTER THE PANOPTICON

For technology to be effective, it doesn't always have to work. Take China's facial-recognition glasses.

Police in the central Chinese city of Zhengzhou recently showed off the specs at a high-speed rail station for state media and others.

They snapped photos of a policewoman peering from behind the shaded lenses.

But the glasses work only if the target stands still for several seconds. They have been used mostly to check travelers for fake identifications.

China's national database of individuals it has flagged for watching — including suspected terrorists, criminals, drug traffickers, political activists and others — includes 20 million to 30 million people, said one technology executive who works closely with the government. That is too many people for today's facial recognition technology to parse, said the executive, who asked not to be identified because the information wasn't public.

The system remains more of a digital patchwork than an all-seeing technological network. Many files still aren't digitized, and others are on mismatched spreadsheets that can't be easily reconciled. Systems that police hope will someday be powered by A.I. are currently run by teams of people sorting through photos and data the old-fashioned way.

Take, for example, the crosswalk in Xiangyang. The images don't appear instantaneously. The billboard often shows jaywalkers from weeks ago, though authorities have recently reduced the lag to about five or six days. Officials said humans still sift through the images to match them to people's identities.

Still, Chinese authorities who are generally mum about security have embarked on a campaign to persuade the country's people that the high-tech security state is already in place.

China's propagandists are fond of stories in which police use facial recognition to spot wanted criminals at events. An article in People's Daily, the Communist Party's official newspaper, covered a series of arrests made with the aid of facial recognition at concerts of the pop star Jackie Cheung. The piece referenced some of the singer's lyrics: "You are a boundless net of love that easily trapped me."

In many places, it works. At the intersection in Xiangyang, jay

GILLES SABRIÉ FOR THE NEW YORK TIMES

An outdoor screen in Xiangyang displays photos of jaywalkers alongside their names and I.D. numbers. The idea is to embarrass offenders into compliance.

walking has decreased. At the building complex where Number 1 Community's facial-recognition gate system has been installed, a problem with bike theft ceased entirely, according to building management.

"The whole point is that people don't know if they're being monitored, and that uncertainty makes people more obedient," said Mr. Chorzempa, the Peterson Institute fellow.

He described the approach as a panopticon, the idea that people will follow the rules precisely because they don't know whether they are being watched.

In Zhengzhou, police were happy to explain how just the thought of the facial recognition glasses could get criminals to confess.

Mr. Shan, the Zhengzhou railway station deputy police chief, cited the time his department grabbed a heroin smuggler. While questioning the suspect, Mr. Shan said, police pulled out the glasses and told the man that what he said didn't matter. The glasses could give them all the information they needed.

"Because he was afraid of being found out by the advanced technology, he confessed," said Mr. Shan, adding that the suspect had swallowed 60 small packs of heroin.

"We didn't even use any interrogation techniques," Mr. Shan said. "He simply gave it all up."

How Tech Giants Are Devising Real Ethics for Artificial Intelligence

BY JOHN MARKOFF | SEPT. 1, 2016

SAN FRANCISCO — For years, science-fiction moviemakers have been making us fear the bad things that artificially intelligent machines might do to their human creators. But for the next decade or two, our biggest concern is more likely to be that robots will take away our jobs or bump into us on the highway.

Now five of the world's largest tech companies are trying to create a standard of ethics around the creation of artificial intelligence. While science fiction has focused on the existential threat of A.I. to humans, researchers at Google's parent company, Alphabet, and those from Amazon, Facebook, IBM and Microsoft have been meeting to discuss more tangible issues, such as the impact of A.I. on jobs, transportation and even warfare.

Tech companies have long overpromised what artificially intelligent machines can do. In recent years, however, the A.I. field has made rapid advances in a range of areas, from self-driving cars and machines that understand speech, like Amazon's Echo device, to a new generation of weapons systems that threaten to automate combat.

The specifics of what the industry group will do or say — even its name — have yet to be hashed out. But the basic intention is clear: to ensure that A.I. research is focused on benefiting people, not hurting them, according to four people involved in the creation of the industry partnership who are not authorized to speak about it publicly.

The importance of the industry effort is underscored in a report issued on Thursday by a Stanford University group funded by Eric Horvitz, a Microsoft researcher who is one of the executives in the industry discussions. The Stanford project, called the One Hundred Year Study on Artificial Intelligence, lays out a plan to produce a detailed report on the impact of A.I. on society every five years for the next century.

One main concern for people in the tech industry would be if regulators jumped in to create rules around their A.I. work. So they are trying to create a framework for a self-policing organization, though it is not clear yet how that will function.

"We're not saying that there should be no regulation," said Peter Stone, a computer scientist at the University of Texas at Austin and one of the authors of the Stanford report. "We're saying that there is a right way and a wrong way."

While the tech industry is known for being competitive, there have been instances when companies have worked together when it was in their best interests. In the 1990s, for example, tech companies agreed on a standard method for encrypting e-commerce transactions, laying the groundwork for two decades of growth in internet business.

The authors of the Stanford report, which is titled "Artificial Intelligence and Life in 2030," argue that it will be impossible to regulate A.I. "The study panel's consensus is that attempts to regulate A.I. in general would be misguided, since there is no clear definition of A.I. (it isn't any one thing), and the risks and considerations are very different in different domains," the report says.

One recommendation in the report is to raise the awareness of and expertise about artificial intelligence at all levels of government, Dr. Stone said. It also calls for increased public and private spending on A.I.

"There is a role for government and we respect that," said David Kenny, general manager for IBM's Watson artificial intelligence division. The challenge, he said, is "a lot of times policies lag the technologies."

A memorandum is being circulated among the five companies with a tentative plan to announce the new organization in the middle of September. One of the unresolved issues is that Google DeepMind, an Alphabet subsidiary, has asked to participate separately, according to a person involved in the negotiations.

The A.I. industry group is modeled on a similar human rights effort known as the Global Network Initiative, in which corporations and nongovernmental organizations are focused on freedom of expression and privacy rights, according to someone briefed by the industry organizers but not authorized to speak about it publicly.

Separately, Reid Hoffman, a founder of LinkedIn who has a background in artificial intelligence, is in discussions with the Massachusetts Institute of Technology Media Lab to fund a project exploring the social and economic effects of artificial intelligence.

Both the M.I.T. effort and the industry partnership are trying to link technology advances more closely to social and economic policy issues. The M.I.T. group has been discussing the idea of designing new A.I. and robotic systems with "society in the loop."

The phrase is a reference to the long-running debate about designing computer and robotic systems that still require interaction with humans. For example, the Pentagon has recently begun articulating a military strategy that calls for using A.I. in which humans continue to control killing decisions, rather than delegating that responsibility to machines.

"The key thing that I would point out is computer scientists have not been good at interacting with the social scientists and the philosophers," said Joichi Ito, the director of the MIT Media Lab and a member of the board of directors of The New York Times. "What we want to do is support and reinforce the social scientists who are doing research which will play a role in setting policies."

The Stanford report attempts to define the issues that citizens of a typical North American city will face in computers and robotic systems that mimic human capabilities. The authors explore eight aspects of modern life, including health care, education, entertainment and employment, but specifically do not look at the issue of warfare. They said that military A.I. applications were outside their current scope and expertise, but they did not rule out focusing on weapons in the future.

The report also does not consider the belief of some computer specialists about the possibility of a "singularity" that might lead to machines that are more intelligent and possibly threaten humans.

"It was a conscious decision not to give credence to this in the report," Dr. Stone said.

How to Regulate Artificial Intelligence

OPINION | BY OREN ETZIONI | SEPT. 1, 2017

THE TECHNOLOGY ENTREPRENEUR Elon Musk recently urged the nation's governors to regulate artificial intelligence "before it's too late." Mr. Musk insists that artificial intelligence represents an "existential threat to humanity," an alarmist view that confuses A.I. science with science fiction. Nevertheless, even A.I. researchers like me recognize that there are valid concerns about its impact on weapons, jobs and privacy. It's natural to ask whether we should develop A.I. at all.

I believe the answer is yes. But shouldn't we take steps to at least slow down progress on A.I., in the interest of caution? The problem is that if we do so, then nations like China will overtake us. The A.I. horse has left the barn, and our best bet is to attempt to steer it. A.I. should not be weaponized, and any A.I. must have an impregnable "off switch." Beyond that, we should regulate the tangible impact of A.I. systems (for example, the safety of autonomous vehicles) rather than trying to define and rein in the amorphous and rapidly developing field of A.I.

I propose three rules for artificial intelligence systems that are inspired by, yet develop further, the "three laws of robotics" that the writer Isaac Asimov introduced in 1942: A robot may not injure a human being or, through inaction, allow a human being to come to harm; a robot must obey the orders given it by human beings, except when such orders would conflict with the previous law; and a robot must protect its own existence as long as such protection does not conflict with the previous two laws.

These three laws are elegant but ambiguous: What, exactly, constitutes harm when it comes to A.I.? I suggest a more concrete basis for avoiding A.I. harm, based on three rules of my own.

First, an A.I. system must be subject to the full gamut of laws that apply to its human operator. This rule would cover private, corporate and government systems. We don't want A.I. to engage in cyberbullying,

ISAAC LAWRENCE/AFP/GETTY IMAGES

"Han the Robot" waits on stage before a discussion about the future of humanity in a demonstration of artificial intelligence by Hanson Robotics at the RISE Technology Conference in Hong Kong in July 2017.

stock manipulation or terrorist threats; we don't want the F.B.I. to release A.I. systems that entrap people into committing crimes. We don't want autonomous vehicles that drive through red lights, or worse, A.I. weapons that violate international treaties.

Our common law should be amended so that we can't claim that our A.I. system did something that we couldn't understand or anticipate. Simply put, "My A.I. did it" should not excuse illegal behavior.

My second rule is that an A.I. system must clearly disclose that it is not human. As we have seen in the case of bots — computer programs that can engage in increasingly sophisticated dialogue with real people — society needs assurances that A.I. systems are clearly labeled as such. In 2016, a bot known as Jill Watson, which served as a teaching assistant for an online course at Georgia Tech, fooled students into thinking it was human. A more serious example is the widespread use of pro-Trump political bots on social media in the days leading up to the 2016 elections, according to researchers at Oxford.

My rule would ensure that people know when a bot is impersonating someone. We have already seen, for example, @DeepDrumpf — a bot that humorously impersonated Donald Trump on Twitter. A.I. systems don't just produce fake tweets; they also produce fake news videos. Researchers at the University of Washington recently released a fake video of former President Barack Obama in which he convincingly appeared to be speaking words that had been grafted onto video of him talking about something entirely different.

My third rule is that an A.I. system cannot retain or disclose confidential information without explicit approval from the source of that information. Because of their exceptional ability to automatically elicit, record and analyze information, A.I. systems are in a prime position to acquire confidential information. Think of all the conversations that Amazon Echo — a "smart speaker" present in an increasing number of homes — is privy to, or the information that your child may inadvertently divulge to a toy such as an A.I. Barbie. Even seemingly innocuous housecleaning robots create maps of your home. That is information you want to make sure you control.

My three A.I. rules are, I believe, sound but far from complete. I introduce them here as a starting point for discussion. Whether or not you agree with Mr. Musk's view about A.I.'s rate of progress and its ultimate impact on humanity (I don't), it is clear that A.I. is coming. Society needs to get ready.

OREN ETZIONI is the chief executive of the Allen Institute for Artificial Intelligence.

Leave A.I. Alone

OPINION | BY ANDREW BURT | JAN. 4, 2018

DECEMBER WAS A BIG MONTH for advocates of regulating artificial intelligence. First, a bipartisan group of senators and representatives introduced the Future of A.I. Act, the first federal bill solely focused on A.I. It would create an advisory committee to make recommendations about A.I. — on topics including the technology's effect on the American work force and strategies to protect the privacy rights of those it impacts. Then the New York City Council approved a first-of-its-kind bill that once signed into law will create a task force to examine its own use of automated decision systems, with the ultimate goal of making its use of algorithms fairer and more transparent.

Perhaps not coincidentally, these efforts also overlap with increasing calls to regulate artificial intelligence along with claims by the likes of Elon Musk and Stephen Hawking that it poses a threat to humanity's literal survival.

But this push for broad legislation to regulate A.I. is premature.

To begin with, even experts can't agree on what, exactly, constitutes artificial intelligence. Take the recent report released by the AI Now Institute, aimed at creating a framework for ethically implementing A.I. While itself focused on A.I., the report also acknowledges that no commonly accepted definition of A.I. exists, which it describes loosely as "a broad assemblage of technologies … that have traditionally relied on human capacities."

"Artificial intelligence" is all too frequently used as a shorthand for software that simply does what humans used to do. But replacing human activity is precisely what new technologies accomplish — spears replaced clubs, wheels replaced feet, the printing press replaced scribes, and so on. What's new about A.I. is that this technology isn't simply replacing human activities, external to our bodies; it's also replacing human decision-making, inside our minds.

The challenges created by this novelty should not obscure the fact that A.I. itself is not one technology, or even one singular development. Regulating an assemblage of technology we can't clearly define is a recipe for poor laws and even worse technology.

Indeed, the challenges A.I. poses aren't entirely new. We've already successfully regulated it in the past — we just didn't call it "artificial intelligence." In the 1960s and 1970s, for example, the financial industry began to rely on complex statistical modeling and huge computerized databases to make credit decisions, automating what had been a more manual process of approving or denying credit to borrowers.

Those ethical and legal challenges associated with these models so captivated the public's attention that in the summer of 1970, Newsweek ran a cover story titled "Is Privacy Dead?" detailing the "massive flanking attack" of computers on modern society. Growing awareness of that threat led to broad appeals that echo modern proposals to regulate A.I. "Eventually we have to set up an agency to regulate the computers," Senator Sam Ervin of North Carolina said in 1970.

But instead of regulating all computers, the government sought a targeted approach tailored to specific problems, passing regulations like the Equal Credit Opportunity Act in 1974. That act was meant to reduce credit discrimination against minority groups and to increase consumers' ability to understand what the models were doing — if consumers didn't like their credit score, thanks to the act they could at least know how it could be improved.

That law and others offer valuable lessons today, illustrating the importance of focusing on specific issues — in this case, transparency in credit decisions — and tailoring their solutions accordingly. Any regulation aimed at the range of systems we call "A.I." should seek to be just as specific.

With the thorny exception of cybersecurity, the way the United States regulatory system has approached information technology is arguably the most successful model for regulating technology in existence — fostering innovation while ensuring that the technology we use doesn't break or seriously jeopardize our safety. The backbone of this approach comprises regulations tailored to the explicit problems created by any given technology.

Within the United States' vast framework of laws and regulatory agencies already lie answers to some of the most vexing challenges created by A.I. In the financial sector, for example, the Federal Reserve enforces a regulation called SR 11-7, which addresses the risks created by the complex algorithms used by today's banks. SR 11-7's solution to those challenges is called "effective challenge," which seeks to embed critical analysis into every stage of an algorithm's life cycle — from thoroughly examining the data used to train the algorithm to explicitly outlining the assumptions underlying the model, and more. While SR 11-7 is among the most detailed attempts at governing the challenges of complex algorithms, it's also one of the most overlooked.

This is not, of course, to suggest that artificial intelligence should never be regulated. But if the past is any guide, treating it as a collection of separate technologies, in separate sectors, is destined to be the most effective way to control the benefits it creates — and the dangers it poses.

ANDREW BURT is chief privacy officer and legal engineer at Immuta, a data management platform for data science, which enables companies to create and manage A.I. and machine learning models.

Artificial Intelligence's 'Black Box' Is Nothing to Fear

OPINION | BY VIJAY PANDE | JAN. 25, 2018

ALONGSIDE THE EXCITEMENT and hype about our growing reliance on artificial intelligence, there's fear about the way the technology works. A recent MIT Technology Review article titled "The Dark Secret at the Heart of AI" warned: "No one really knows how the most advanced algorithms do what they do. That could be a problem." Thanks to this uncertainty and lack of accountability, a report by the AI Now Institute recommended that public agencies responsible for criminal justice, health care, welfare and education shouldn't use such technology.

Given these types of concerns, the unseeable space between where data goes in and answers come out is often referred to as a "black box" — seemingly a reference to the hardy (and in fact orange, not black) data recorders mandated on aircraft and often examined after accidents. In the context of A.I., the term more broadly suggests an image of being in the "dark" about how the technology works: We put in and provide the data and models and architectures, and then computers provide us answers while continuing to learn on their own, in a way that's seemingly impossible — and certainly too complicated — for us to understand.

There's particular concern about this in health care, where A.I. is used to classify which skin lesions are cancerous, to identify very early-stage cancer from blood, to predict heart disease, to determine what compounds in people and animals could extend healthy life spans and more. But these fears about the implications of black box are misplaced. A.I. is no less transparent than the way in which doctors have always worked — and in many cases it represents an improvement, augmenting what hospitals can do for patients and the entire health care system. After all, the black box in A.I. isn't a new problem due to new tech: Human intelligence itself is — and always has been — a black box.

Let's take the example of a human doctor making a diagnosis. Afterward, a patient might ask that doctor how she made that diagnosis, and she would probably share some of the data she used to draw her conclusion. But could she really explain how and why she made that decision, what specific data from what studies she drew on, what observations from her training or mentors influenced her, what tacit knowledge she gleaned from her own and her colleagues' shared experiences and how all of this combined into that precise insight? Sure, she'd probably give a few indicators about what pointed her in a certain direction — but there would also be an element of guessing, of following hunches. And even if there weren't, we still wouldn't know that there weren't other factors involved of which she wasn't even consciously aware.

If the same diagnosis had been made with A.I., we could draw from all available information on that particular patient — as well as data anonymously aggregated across time and from countless other relevant patients everywhere, to make the strongest evidence-based decision possible. It would be a diagnosis with a direct connection to the data, rather than human intuition based on limited data and derivative summaries of anecdotal experiences with a relatively small number of local patients.

But we make decisions in areas that we don't fully understand every day — often very successfully — from the predicted economic impacts of policies to weather forecasts to the ways in which we approach much of science in the first place. We either oversimplify things or accept that they're too complex for us to break down linearly, let alone explain fully. It's just like the black box of A.I.: Human intelligence can reason and make arguments for a given conclusion, but it can't explain the complex, underlying basis for how we arrived at a particular conclusion. Think of what happens when a couple get divorced because of one stated cause — say, infidelity — when in reality there's an entire unseen universe of intertwined causes, forces and events that contributed to that outcome. Why did they choose to split

XINHUA/THEN CHIH WEY/GETTY IMAGES

A prosthetic arm displayed at an exhibit about science and technology changing perceptions of humanity.

up when another couple in a similar situation didn't? Even those in the relationship can't fully explain it. It's a black box.

The irony is that compared with human intelligence, A.I. is actually the more transparent of intelligences. Unlike the human mind, A.I. can — and should — be interrogated and interpreted. Like the ability to audit and refine models and expose knowledge gaps in deep neural nets and the debugging tools that will inevitably be built and the potential ability to augment human intelligence via brain-computer interfaces, there are many technologies that could help interpret artificial intelligence in a way we can't interpret the human brain. In the process, we may even learn more about how human intelligence itself works.

Perhaps the real source of critics' concerns isn't that we can't "see" A.I.'s reasoning but that as A.I. gets more powerful, the human mind becomes the limiting factor. It's that in the future, we'll need A.I. to understand A.I. In health care as well as in other fields, this means we will soon see the creation of a category of human professionals who don't have to make the moment-to-moment decisions themselves but instead manage a team of A.I. workers — just like commercial airplane pilots who engage autopilots to land in poor weather conditions. Doctors will no longer "drive" the primary diagnosis; instead, they'll ensure that the diagnosis is relevant and meaningful for a patient and oversee when and how to offer more clarification and more narrative explanation. The doctor's office of the future will very likely include computer assistants, on both the doctor's side and the patient's side, as well as data inputs that come from far beyond the office walls.

When that happens, it will become clear that the so-called black box of artificial intelligence is more of a feature, not a bug — because it's more possible to capture and explain what's going on there than it is in the human mind. None of this dismisses or ignores the need for oversight of A.I. It's just that instead of worrying about the black box, we should focus on the opportunity and therefore better address a future where A.I. not only augments human intelligence and intuition but also perhaps even sheds light on and redefines what it means to be human in the first place.

VIJAY PANDE is a general partner in Andreessen Horowitz, a venture capital firm that invests in companies at the intersection of biology and computer science, including A.I. companies. He is a former director of the biophysics program at Stanford University.

CHAPTER 4

Philosophical Reflections

This chapter presents writing by prominent thinkers that reflect on artificial intelligence. All of these essays were originally published in The Stone, a New York Times "forum for contemporary philosophers and other thinkers on issues both timely and timeless." The series is edited by Simon Critchley, a professor of philosophy at the New School for Social Research in New York. Among the diverse ideas considered by these essays are the possibility of building artificial moral agents, human being's moral obligations to A.I. and the possibilities for real affection between humans and A.I.

The Future of Moral Machines

OPINION | BY COLIN ALLEN | DEC. 25, 2011

A ROBOT WALKS INTO A BAR and says, "I'll have a screwdriver." A bad joke, indeed. But even less funny if the robot says "Give me what's in your cash register."

The fictional theme of robots turning against humans is older than the word itself, which first appeared in the title of Karel Čapek's 1920 play about artificial factory workers rising against their human overlords. Just 22 years later, Isaac Asimov invented the "Three Laws of Robotics" to serve as a hierarchical ethical code for the robots in his stories: first, never harm a human being through action or inaction; second, obey human orders; last, protect oneself. From the first story in which the laws appeared, Asimov explored their inherent contradictions. Great fiction, but unworkable theory.

Machines are increasingly operating with minimal human oversight in the same physical spaces as we do.

The prospect of machines capable of following moral principles, let alone understanding them, seems as remote today as the word "robot" is old. Some technologists enthusiastically extrapolate from the observation that computing power doubles every 18 months to predict an imminent "technological singularity" in which a threshold for machines of superhuman intelligence will be suddenly surpassed. Many Singularitarians assume a lot, not the least of which is that intelligence is fundamentally a computational process. The techno-optimists among them also believe that such machines will be essentially friendly to human beings. I am skeptical about the Singularity, and even if "artificial intelligence" is not an oxymoron, "friendly A.I." will require considerable scientific progress on a number of fronts.

The neuro- and cognitive sciences are presently in a state of rapid development in which alternatives to the metaphor of mind as computer have gained ground. Dynamical systems theory, network science, statistical learning theory, developmental psychobiology and molecular neuroscience all challenge some foundational assumptions of A.I., and the last 50 years of cognitive science more generally. These new approaches analyze and exploit the complex causal structure of physically embodied and environmentally embedded systems, at every level, from molecular to social. They demonstrate the inadequacy of highly abstract algorithms operating on discrete symbols with fixed meanings to capture the adaptive flexibility of intelligent behavior. But despite undermining the idea that the mind is fundamentally a digital computer, these approaches have improved our ability to use computers for more and more robust simulations of intelligent agents — simulations that will increasingly control machines occupying our cognitive niche. If you don't believe me, ask Siri.

This is why, in my view, we need to think long and hard about machine morality. Many of my colleagues take the very idea of moral machines to be a kind of joke. Machines, they insist, do only what they are told to do. A bar-robbing robot would have to be instructed or constructed to do exactly that. On this view, morality is an issue only for creatures like us who can choose to do wrong. People are morally good only insofar as they must overcome the urge to do what is bad. We can be moral, they say, because we are free to choose our own paths.

There are big themes here: freedom of will, human spontaneity and creativity, and the role of reason in making good choices — not to mention the nature of morality itself. Fully human-level moral agency, and all the responsibilities that come with it, requires developments in artificial intelligence or artificial life that remain, for now, in the domain of science fiction. And yet…

Machines are increasingly operating with minimal human oversight in the same physical spaces as we do. Entrepreneurs are actively developing robots for home care of the elderly. Robotic vacuum cleaners and lawn mowers are already mass market items. Self-driving cars are not far behind. Mercedes is equipping its 2013 model S-Class cars with a system that can drive autonomously through city traffic at speeds up to 25 m.p.h. Google's fleet of autonomous cars has logged about 200,000 miles without incident in California and Nevada, in conditions ranging from surface streets to freeways. By Google's estimate, the cars have required intervention by a human co-pilot only about once every 1,000 miles and the goal is to reduce this rate to once in 1,000,000 miles. How long until the next bank robber will have an autonomous getaway vehicle?

This is autonomy in the engineer's sense, not the philosopher's. The cars won't have a sense of free will, not even an illusory one. They may select their own routes through the city but, for the foreseeable future, they won't choose their own paths in the grand journey from dealership to junkyard. We don't want our cars leaving us to join the Peace Corps, nor will they any time soon. But as the layers of software pile up between us and our machines, they are becoming increasingly independent of our direct control. In military circles, the phrase "man on the loop" has come to replace "man in the loop," indicating the diminishing role of human overseers in controlling drones and ground-based robots that operate hundreds or thousands of miles from base. These machines need to adjust to local conditions faster than can be signaled and processed by human tele-operators. And while no one is yet recommending that decisions to use lethal force should be handed over to software, the Department of Defense is sufficiently committed to the use of autonomous systems that it has sponsored engineers and philosophers to outline prospects for ethical governance of battlefield machines.

Joke or not, the topic of machine morality is here to stay. Even modest amounts of engineered autonomy make it necessary to outline some modest goals for the design of artificial moral agents. Modest because we are not talking about guidance systems for the Terminator or other technology that does not yet exist. Necessary, because as machines with limited autonomy operate more often than before in open environments, it becomes increasingly important to design a kind of functional morality that is sensitive to ethically relevant features of those situations. Modest, again, because this functional morality is not about self-reflective moral agency — what one might call "full" moral agency — but simply about trying to make autonomous agents better at adjusting their actions to human norms. This can be done with technology that is already available or can be anticipated within the next 5 to 10 years.

The project of designing artificial moral agents provokes a wide variety of negative reactions, including that it is preposterous, horrendous, or trivial. My co-author Wendell Wallach and I have been accused of being, in our book "Moral Machines," unimaginatively human-centered in our views about morality, of being excessively optimistic about technological solutions, and of putting too much emphasis on engineering the machines themselves rather than looking at the whole context in which machines operate.

In response to the charge of preposterousness, I am willing to double down. Far from being an exercise in science fiction, serious engagement with the project of designing artificial moral agents has the potential to revolutionize moral philosophy in the same way that philosophers' engagement with science continuously revolutionizes human self-understanding. New insights can be gained from confronting the question of whether and how a control architecture for robots might utilize (or ignore) general principles recommended by major ethical theories. Perhaps ethical theory is to moral agents as physics is to outfielders — theoretical knowledge that isn't necessary to play a good game. Such theoretical knowledge may still be useful after the fact to analyze and adjust future performance.

Even if success in building artificial moral agents will be hard to gauge, the effort may help to forestall inflexible, ethically-blind technologies from propagating. More concretely, if cars are smart enough to navigate through city traffic, they are certainly smart enough to detect how long they have been parked outside a bar (easily accessible through the marriage of G.P.S. and the Internet) and to ask you, the driver, to prove you're not drunk before starting the engine so you can get home. For the near term (say, 5 to 10 years), a responsible human will still be needed to supervise these "intelligent" cars, so you had better be sober. Does this really require artificial morality, when one could simply put a breathalyzer between key and ignition? Such a dumb, inflexible system would have a kind of operational morality in which the engineer has decided that no car should be started by person with a certain blood alcohol level. But it would be ethically blind — incapable, for instance, of recognizing the difference between, on the one hand, a driver who needs the car simply to get home and, on the other hand, a driver who had a couple of drinks with dinner but needs the car because a 4-year-old requiring urgent medical attention is in the back seat.

It is within our current capacities to build machines that are able to determine, based on real-time information about current traffic conditions and access to actuarial tables, how likely it is that this situation might lead to an accident. Of course, this only defers the ethical question of how to weigh the potential for harm that either option presents, but a well-designed system of human-machine interaction could allow for a manual override to be temporarily logged in a "black-box" similar to those used on airplanes. In case of an accident this would provide evidence that the person had taken responsibility. Just as we can envisage machines with increasing degrees of autonomy from human oversight, we can envisage machines whose controls involve increasing degrees of sensitivity to things that matter ethically. Not perfect machines, to be sure, but better.

DOES THIS TALK of artificial moral agents overreach, contributing to our own dehumanization, to the reduction of human autonomy, and to lowered barriers to warfare? If so, does it grease the slope to a horrendous, dystopian future? I am sensitive to the worries, but optimistic enough to think that this kind of techno-pessimism has, over the centuries, been oversold. Luddites have always come to seem quaint, except when they were dangerous. The challenge for philosophers and engineers alike is to figure out what should and can reasonably be done in the middle space that contains somewhat autonomous, partly ethically-sensitive machines. Some may think the exploration of this space is too dangerous to allow. Prohibitionists may succeed in some areas — robot arms control, anyone? — but they will not, I believe, be able to contain the spread of increasingly autonomous robots into homes, eldercare, and public spaces, not to mention the virtual spaces in which much software already operates without a human in the loop. We want machines that do chores and errands without our having to monitor them continuously. Retailers and banks depend on software controlling all manner of operations, from credit card purchases to inventory control, freeing humans to do other things that we don't yet know how to construct machines to do.

Where's the challenge, a software engineer might ask? Isn't ethical governance for machines just problem-solving within constraints?

If there's fuzziness about the nature of those constraints, isn't that a philosophical problem, not an engineering one? Besides, why look to human ethics to provide a gold standard for machines? My response is that if engineers leave it to philosophers to come up with theories that they can implement, they will have a long wait, but if philosophers leave it to engineers to implement something workable they will likely be disappointed by the outcome. The challenge is to reconcile these two rather different ways of approaching the world, to yield better understanding of how interactions among people and contexts enable us, sometimes, to steer a reasonable course through the competing demands of our moral niche. The different kinds of rigor provided by philosophers and engineers are both needed to inform the construction of machines that, when embedded in well-designed systems of human-machine interaction, produce morally reasonable decisions even in situations where Asimov's laws would produce deadlock.

COLIN ALLEN directs the Program in Cognitive Science at Indiana University, Bloomington, where he is Provost Professor of Cognitive Science and History and Philosophy of Science. He works on animal cognition, philosophical foundations of cognitive science and computing applications for philosophy.

Cambridge, Cabs and Copenhagen: My Route to Existential Risk

OPINION | BY HUW PRICE | JAN. 27, 2013

IN COPENHAGEN the summer before last, I shared a taxi with a man who thought his chance of dying in an artificial intelligence-related accident was as high as that of heart disease or cancer. No surprise if he'd been the driver, perhaps (never tell a taxi driver that you're a philosopher!), but this was a man who has spent his career with computers.

Indeed, he's so talented in that field that he is one of the team who made this century so, well, 21st — who got us talking to one another on video screens, the way we knew we'd be doing in the 21st century, back when I was a boy, half a century ago. For this was Jaan Tallinn, one of the team who gave us Skype. (Since then, taking him to dinner in Trinity College here in Cambridge, I've had colleagues queuing up to shake his hand, thanking him for keeping them in touch with distant grandchildren.)

There could be trouble when intelligence escapes the constraints of biology.

I knew of the suggestion that A.I. might be dangerous, of course. I had heard of the "singularity," or "intelligence explosion" — roughly, the idea, originally due to the statistician I J Good (a Cambridge-trained former colleague of Alan Turing's), that once machine intelligence reaches a certain point, it could take over its own process of improvement, perhaps exponentially, so that we humans would soon be left far behind. But I'd never met anyone who regarded it as such a pressing cause for concern — let alone anyone with their feet so firmly on the ground in the software business.

I was intrigued, and also impressed, by Tallinn's commitment to doing something about it. The topic came up because I'd asked what he worked on these days. The answer, in part, is that he spends a lot of his time trying to improve the odds, in one way or another (talking to philosophers in Danish taxis, for example).

I was heading for Cambridge at the time, to take up my new job as Bertrand Russell professor of philosophy — a chair named after a man who spent the last years of his life trying to protect humanity from another kind of technological risk, that of nuclear war. And one of the people I already knew in Cambridge was the distinguished cosmologist Martin Rees — then master of Trinity College, and former president of the Royal Society. Lord Rees is another outspoken proponent of the view that we humans should pay more attention to the ways in which our own technology might threaten our survival. (Biotechnology gets most attention, in his work.)

So it occurred to me that there might be a useful, interesting and appropriate role for me, as a kind of catalyst between these two activists, and their respective circles. And that, to fast forward a little, is how I came to be taking Jaan Tallinn to dinner in Trinity College; and how he, Martin Rees and I now come to be working together, to establish here in Cambridge the Centre for the Study of Existential Risk (C.S.E.R.).

By "existential risks" (E.R.) we mean, roughly, catastrophic risks to our species that are "our fault," in the sense that they arise from human technologies. These are not the only catastrophic risks we humans face, of course: asteroid impacts and extreme volcanic events could wipe us out, for example. But in comparison with possible technological risks, these natural risks are comparatively well studied and, arguably, comparatively minor (the major source of uncertainty being on the technological side). So the greatest need, in our view, is to pay a lot more attention to these technological risks. That's why we chose to make them the explicit focus of our center.

I have now met many fascinating scholars — scientists, philosophers and others — who think that these issues are profoundly important, and seriously understudied. Strikingly, though, they differ about where they think the most pressing risks lie. A Cambridge zoologist I met recently is most worried about deadly designer bacteria, produced — whether by error or by terror, as Rees puts it — in a nearby future in which there's almost an app for such things. To him, A.I. risk seemed comparatively far-fetched — though he confessed that he was no expert (and added that the evidence is that even experts do little better than chance, in many areas).

Where do I stand on the A.I. case, the one that got me into this business? I don't claim any great expertise on the matter (perhaps wisely, in the light of the evidence just mentioned). For what it's worth, however, my view goes like this. On the one hand, I haven't yet seen a strong case for being quite as pessimistic as Jaan Tallinn was in the taxi that day. (To be fair, he himself says that he's not always that pessimistic.) On the other hand, I do think that there are strong reasons to think that we humans are nearing one of the most significant moments in our entire history: the point at which intelligence escapes the constraints of biology. And I see no compelling grounds for confidence that if that does happen, we will survive the transition in reasonable shape. Without such grounds, I think we have cause for concern.

My case for these conclusions relies on three main observations. The first is that our own intelligence is an evolved biological solution to a kind of optimization problem, operating under very tight constraints of time, energy, raw materials, historical starting point and no doubt many other factors. The hardware needs to fit through a mammalian birth canal, to be reasonably protected for a mobile life in a hazardous environment, to consume something like 1,000 calories per day and so on — not to mention being achievable by mutation and selection over a time scale of some tens of millions of years, starting from what existed back then!

Second, this biological endowment, such as it is, has been essentially constant, for many thousands of years. It is a kind of fixed point in the landscape, a mountain peak on which we have all lived for hundreds of generations. Think of it as Mount Fuji, for example. We are creatures of this volcano. The fact that it towers above the surrounding landscape enables us to dominate our environment and accounts for our extraordinary success, compared with most other species on the planet. (Some species benefit from our success, of course: cockroaches and rats, perhaps, and the many distinctive bacteria that inhabit our guts.) And the distinctive shape of the peak — also constant, or nearly so, for all these generations — is very deeply entangled with our sense of what it is to be us. We are not just creatures of any volcano; we are creatures of this one.

Both the height and the shape of the mountain are products of our biological history, in the main. (The qualification is needed because cultural inheritance may well play a role too.) Our great success in the biological landscape, in turn, is mainly because of the fact that the distinctive intelligence that the height and shape represent has enabled us to control and modify the surrounding environment. We've been exercising such control for a very long time of course, but we've recently got much better at it. Modern science and technology give us new and extraordinarily powerful ways to modify the natural world, and the creatures of the ancient volcano are more dominant than ever before.

This is all old news, of course, as is the observation that this success may ultimately be our undoing. (Remember Malthus.) But the new concern, linked to speculation about the future of A.I., is that we may soon be in a position to do something entirely new: to unleash a kind of artificial vulcanism, that may change the shape and height of our own mountain, or build new ones, perhaps even higher, and perhaps of shapes we cannot presently imagine. In other words — and this is my third observation — we face the prospect that designed non-biological technologies, operating under entirely different constraints in many respects, may soon do the kinds of things that our brain does, but very much faster, and very much better, in whatever dimensions of improvement may turn out to be available.

The claim that we face this prospect may seem contestable. Is it really plausible that technology will reach this stage (ever, let alone soon)? I'll come back to this. For the moment, the point I want to make is simply that if we do suppose that we are going to reach such a stage — a point at which technology reshapes our human Mount Fuji, or builds other peaks elsewhere — then it's not going to be business as usual, as far as we are concerned. Technology will have modified the one thing, more than anything else, that has made it "business as usual" so long as we have been human.

Indeed, it's not really clear who "we" would be, in those circumstances. Would we be humans surviving (or not) in an environment in which superior machine intelligences had taken the reins, to speak? Would we be human intelligences somehow extended by nonbiological means? Would we be in some sense entirely posthuman (though thinking of ourselves perhaps as descendants of humans)? I don't claim that these are the only options, or even that these options are particularly well formulated — they're not! My point is simply that if technology does get to this stage, the most important fixed point in our landscape is no longer fixed — on the contrary, it might be moving, rapidly, in directions we creatures of the volcano are not well equipped to understand, let alone predict. That seems to me a cause for concern.

These are my reasons for thinking that at some point over the horizon, there's a major tipping point awaiting us, when intelligence escapes its biological constraints; and that it is far from clear that that's good news, from our point of view. To sum it up briefly, the argument rests on three propositions: (i) the level and general shape of human intelligence is highly contingent, a product of biological constraints and accidents; (ii) despite its contingency in the big scheme of things, it is essential to us — it is who we are, more or less, and it accounts for our success; (iii) technology is likely to give us the means to bypass the biological constraints, either altering our own minds or constructing machines with comparable capabilities, and thereby reforming the landscape.

But how far away might this tipping point be, and will it ever happen at all? This brings me back to the most contested claim of these three — the assertion that nonbiological machines are likely, at some point, to be as intelligent or more intelligent than the "biological machines" we have in our skulls.

Objections to this claim come from several directions. Some contest it based on the (claimed) poor record of A.I. so far; others on the basis of some claimed fundamental difference between human minds and computers; yet others, perhaps, on the grounds that the claim is simply unclear — it isn't clear what intelligence is, for example.

To arguments of the last kind, I'm inclined to give a pragmatist's answer: Don't think about what intelligence is, think about what it does. Putting it rather crudely, the distinctive thing about our peak in the present biological landscape is that we tend to be much better at controlling our environment than any other species. In these terms, the question is then whether machines might at some point do an even better job (perhaps a vastly better job). If so, then all the above concerns seem to be back on the table, even though we haven't mentioned the word "intelligence," let alone tried to say what it means. (You might try to resurrect the objection by focusing on the word "control," but here I think you'd be on thin ice: it's clear that machines already control things, in some sense — they drive cars, for example.)

I see no good reason to believe that intelligence is never going to escape from the head.

Much the same point can be made against attempts to take comfort in the idea that there is something fundamentally different between human minds and computers. Suppose there is, and that that means that computers will never do some of the things that we do — write philosophy, appreciate the sublime, or whatever. What's the case for thinking that without these gifts, the machines cannot control the terrestrial environment a lot more effectively than we do?

People who worry about these things often say that the main threat may come from accidents involving "dumb optimizers" — machines with rather simple goals (producing IKEA furniture, say) that figure out that they can improve their output astronomically by taking control of various resources on which we depend for our survival. Nobody expects an automated furniture factory to do philosophy. Does that make it less dangerous? (Would you bet your grandchildren's lives on the matter?)

But there's a more direct answer, too, to this attempt to take comfort in any supposed difference between human minds and computers. It also cuts against attempts to take refuge in the failure of A.I. to live up to some of its own hype. It's an answer in two parts. The first part — let me call it, a little aggressively, the blow to the head — points out that however biology got us onto this exalted peak in the landscape, the tricks are all there for our inspection: most of it is done with the glop inside our skulls. Understand that, and you understand how to do it artificially, at least in principle. Sure, it could turn out that there's then no way to improve things — that biology, despite all the constraints, really has hit some sort of fundamental maximum. Or it could turn out that the task of figuring out how biology did it is just beyond us, at least for the foreseeable future (even the remotely foreseeable future). But again, are you going to bet your grandchildren on that possibility?

The second part of the argument — the blow from below — asks these opponents just how far up the intelligence mountain they think that A.I. could get us. To the level of our fishy ancestors? Our early mammalian ancestors? (Keep in mind that the important question is the pragmatic one: Could a machine do what these creatures do?) Wherever they claim to draw the line, the objection challenges them to say what biology does next, that no nonbiological machine could possibly do. Perhaps someone has a plausible answer to this question, but for my part, I have no idea what it could be.

At present, then, I see no good reason to believe that intelligence is never going to escape from the head, or that it won't do so in time scales we could reasonably care about. Hence it seems to me eminently sensible to think about what happens if and when it does so, and whether there's something we can do to favor good outcomes over bad, in that case. That's how I see what Rees, Tallinn and I want to do in Cambridge (about this kind of technological risk, as about others): we're trying to assemble an organization that will use the combined intellectual power of a lot of gifted people to shift some probability from the bad side to the good.

Tallin compares this to wearing a seat belt. Most of us agree that that makes sense, even if the risk of an accident is low, and even though we can't be certain that it would be beneficial, if we were to have an accident. (Occasionally, seat belts make things worse.) The analogy is apt in another way, too. It is easy to turn a blind eye to the case for wearing a seat belt. Many of us don't wear them in taxis, for example. Something — perhaps optimism, a sense that caution isn't cool, or (if you're sufficiently English!) a misplaced concern about hurting the driver's feelings — just gets in the way of the simple choice to put the thing on. Usually it makes no difference, of course, but sometimes people get needlessly hurt.

Worrying about catastrophic risk may have similar image problems. We tend to be optimists, and it might be easier, and perhaps in some sense cooler, not to bother. So I finish with two recommendations. First, keep in mind that in this case our fate is in the hands, if that's the word, of what might charitably be called a very large and poorly organized committee — collectively shortsighted, if not actually reckless, but responsible for guiding our fast-moving vehicle through some hazardous and yet completely unfamiliar terrain. Second, remember that all the children — all of them — are in the back. We thrill-seeking grandparents may have little to lose, but shouldn't we be encouraging the kids to buckle up?

HUW PRICE is Bertrand Russell professor of philosophy at the University of Cambridge. With Martin Rees and Jaan Tallinn, he is a co-founder of the project to establish the Centre for the Study of Existential Risk.

The Philosophy of 'Her'

OPINION | BY SUSAN SCHNEIDER | MARCH 2, 2014

> *You know, I actually used to be so worried about not having a body, but now I truly love it ... I'm not tethered to time and space in the way that I would be if I was stuck inside a body that's inevitably going to die. — Samantha, in "Her"*

SET IN THE not-too-distant future, Spike Jonze's film "Her" explores the romantic relationship between Samantha, a computer program, and Theodore Twombly, a human being. Though Samantha is not human, she feels the pangs of heartbreak, intermittently longs for a body and is bewildered by her own evolution. She has a rich inner life, complete with experiences and sensations.

"Her" raises two questions that have long preoccupied philosophers. Are nonbiological creatures like Samantha capable of consciousness — at least in theory, if not yet in practice? And if so, does that mean that we humans might one day be able to upload our own minds to computers, perhaps to join Samantha in being untethered from "a body that's inevitably going to die"?

Might we humans be able to upload our minds to computers, perhaps to join our digital lovers in the virtual universe?

This is not mere speculation. The Future of Humanity Institute at Oxford University has released a report on the technological requirements for uploading a mind to a machine. A Defense Department agency has funded a program, Synapse, that is trying to develop a computer that resembles a brain in form and function. The futurist Ray Kurzweil, now a director of engineering at Google, has even discussed the potential advantages of forming friendships, "Her"-style, with personalized artificial intelligence systems. He and others contend that we are fast approaching the "technological singularity," a point at which artificial intelligence, or A.I., surpasses human intelligence, with unpredictable consequences for civilization and human nature.

Is all of this really possible? Not everyone thinks so. Some people argue that the capacity to be conscious is unique to biological organisms, so that even superintelligent A.I. programs would be devoid of conscious experience. If this view is correct, then a relationship between a human being and a program like Samantha, however intelligent she might be, would be hopelessly one-sided. Moreover, few humans would want to join Samantha, for to upload your brain to a computer would be to forfeit your consciousness.

This view, however, has been steadily losing ground. Its opponents point out that our best empirical theory of the brain holds that it is an information-processing system and that all mental functions are computations. If this is right, then creatures like Samantha can be conscious, for they have the same kind of minds as ours: computational ones. Just as a phone call and a smoke signal can convey the same information, thought can have both silicon- and carbon-based substrates. Indeed, scientists have produced silicon-based artificial neurons that can exchange information with real neurons. The neural code increasingly seems to be a computational one.

You might worry that we could never be certain that programs like Samantha were conscious. This concern is akin to the longstanding philosophical conundrum known as the "problem of other minds." The problem is that although you can know that you yourself are conscious, you cannot know for sure that other people are. You might, after all, be witnessing behavior with no accompanying conscious component.

In the face of the problem of other minds, all you can do is note that other people have brains that are structurally similar to your own and conclude that since you yourself are conscious, others are likely to be conscious as well. When confronted with a high-level A.I. program like Samantha, your predicament wouldn't be all that different, especially if that program had been engineered to work like the human brain. While we couldn't be certain that an A.I. program genuinely felt anything, we can't be certain that other humans do, either. But it would seem probable in both cases.

If the Samanthas of the future will have inner lives like ours, however, I suspect that we will not be able to upload ourselves to computers to join them in the digital universe. To see why, imagine that Theodore wants to upload himself. Imagine, furthermore, that uploading involves (a) scanning a human brain in such exacting detail that it destroys the original and (b) creating a software model that thinks and behaves in precisely the same way as the original did. If Theodore were to undergo this procedure, would he succeed in transferring himself into the digital realm? Or would he, as I suspect, succeed only in killing himself, leaving behind a computational copy of his mind — one that, adding insult to injury, would date his girlfriend?

Ordinary physical objects follow a continuous path through space over time. For Theodore to transfer his mind into a computer program, however, his mind would not follow a continuous trajectory. His brain would be destroyed when the scan was made, and the information about his precise brain configuration would be sent to a computer, which could be miles away.

Furthermore, if Theodore were to truly upload his mind (as opposed to merely copy its contents), then he could be downloaded to multiple other computers. Suppose that there are five such downloads: Which one is the real Theodore? It is hard to provide a nonarbitrary answer. Could all of the downloads be Theodore? This seems bizarre: As a rule, physical objects and living things do not occupy multiple locations at once. It is far more likely that none of the downloads are Theodore, and that he did not upload in the first place.

Worse yet, imagine that the scanning procedure doesn't destroy Theodore's brain, so the original Theodore survives. If he survives the scan, why conclude that his consciousness has transferred to the computer? It should still reside in his brain. But if you believe that his mind doesn't transfer if his brain isn't destroyed, then why believe that his mind does transfer if his brain is destroyed?

It is here that we press up against the boundaries of the digital universe. It seems there is a categorical divide between humans and programs: Humans cannot upload themselves to the digital universe; they can upload only copies of themselves — copies that may themselves be conscious beings.

Does this mean that uploading projects should be scrapped? I don't think so, for uploading technology can benefit our species. A global catastrophe may make the world inhospitable to biological life forms, and uploading may be the only way to preserve the human way of life and thinking, if not actual humans themselves. And uploading could facilitate the development of brain therapies and enhancements that can benefit humans and nonhuman animals. Furthermore, uploading may give rise to a form of superintelligent A.I. A.I. that is descended from us may have greater chance of being benevolent toward us.

Finally, some humans will understandably want digital backups of themselves. What if you found out that you were going to die soon? A desire to contribute a backup copy of yourself might outweigh your desire to spend a few more days on the planet. Or you might wish to leave a copy of yourself to communicate with your children or complete projects that you care about. Indeed, the Samanthas of the future might be uploaded copies of deceased humans we have loved deeply. Or perhaps our best friends will be copies of ourselves, but tweaked in ways we find insightful.

SUSAN SCHNEIDER, an associate professor of philosophy at the University of Connecticut, is the author of "The Language of Thought" and "Science Fiction and Philosophy."

Outing A.I.: Beyond the Turing Test

OPINION | BY BENJAMIN H. BRATTON | FEB. 23, 2015

ARTIFICIAL INTELLIGENCE (A.I.) is having a moment, albeit one marked by crucial ambiguities.

Cognoscenti including Stephen Hawking, Elon Musk and Bill Gates, among others, have recently weighed in on its potential and perils. After reading Nick Bostrom's book "Superintelligence," Musk even wondered aloud if A.I. may be "our biggest existential threat."

Our popular conception of artificial intelligence is distorted by an anthropocentric fallacy.

Positions on A.I. are split, and not just on its dangers. Some insist that "hard A.I." (with human-level intelligence) can never exist, while others conclude that it is inevitable. But in many cases these debates may be missing the real point of what it means to live and think with forms of synthetic intelligence very different from our own.

That point, in short, is that a mature A.I. is not necessarily a humanlike intelligence, or one that is at our disposal. If we look for A.I. in the wrong ways, it may emerge in forms that are needlessly difficult to recognize, amplifying its risks and retarding its benefits.

This is not just a concern for the future. A.I. is already out of the lab and deep into the fabric of things. "Soft A.I.," such as Apple's Siri and Amazon recommendation engines, along with infrastructural A.I., such as high-speed algorithmic trading, smart vehicles and industrial robotics, are increasingly a part of everyday life — part of how our tools work, how our cities move and how our economy builds and trades things.

Unfortunately, the popular conception of A.I., at least as depicted in countless movies, games and books, still seems to assume that humanlike characteristics (anger, jealousy, confusion, avarice, pride, desire, not to mention cold alienation) are the most important ones to be on the lookout for. This anthropocentric fallacy may contradict the implications of contemporary A.I. research, but it is still a prism through which much of our culture views an encounter with advanced synthetic cognition.

The little boy robot in Steven Spielberg's 2001 film "A.I. Artificial Intelligence" wants to be a real boy with all his little metal heart, while Skynet in the "Terminator" movies is obsessed with the genocide of humans. We automatically presume that the Monoliths in Stanley Kubrick and Arthur C. Clarke's 1968 film, "2001: A Space Odyssey," want to talk to the human protagonist Dave, and not to his spaceship's A.I., HAL 9000.

I argue that we should abandon the conceit that a "true" Artificial Intelligence must care deeply about humanity — us specifically — as its focus and motivation. Perhaps what we really fear, even more than a Big Machine that wants to kill us, is one that sees us as irrelevant. Worse than being seen as an enemy is not being seen at all.

Unless we assume that humanlike intelligence represents all possible forms of intelligence — a whopper of an assumption — why define an advanced A.I. by its resemblance to ours? After all, "intelligence" is notoriously difficult to define, and human intelligence simply can't exhaust the possibilities. Granted, doing so may at times have practical value in the laboratory, but in cultural terms it is self-defeating, unethical and perhaps even dangerous.

We need a popular culture of A.I. that is less parochial and narcissistic, one that is based on more than simply looking for a machine version of our own reflection. As a basis for staging encounters between various A.I.s and humans, that would be a deeply flawed precondition for communication. Needless to say, our historical track record with "first contacts," even among ourselves, does not provide clear comfort that we are well-prepared.

THE IDEA OF measuring A.I. by its ability to "pass" as a human — dramatized in countless sci-fi films, from Ridley Scott's "Blade Runner" to Spike Jonze's "Her" — is actually as old as modern A.I. research itself.

It is traceable at least to 1950 when the British mathematician Alan Turing published "Computing Machinery and Intelligence," a paper in which he described what we now call the "Turing Test," and which he referred to as the "imitation game." There are different versions of the test, all of which are revealing as to why our approach to the culture and ethics of A.I. is what it is, for good and bad. For the most familiar version, a human interrogator asks questions of two hidden contestants, one a human and the other a computer. Turing suggests that if the interrogator usually cannot tell which is which, and if the computer can successfully pass as human, then can we not conclude, for practical purposes, that the computer is "intelligent"?

There is a correspondence between asking an A.I. to "pass" the test in order to qualify as intelligent — to "pass" as a human intelligence — with Turing's own need to hide his homosexuality and to "pass" as a straight man.

More people "know" Turing's foundational text than have actually read it. This is unfortunate because the text is marvelous, strange and surprising. Turing introduces his test as a variation on a popular parlor game in which two hidden contestants, a woman (player A) and a man (player B) try to convince a third that he or she is a woman by their written responses to leading questions. To win, one of the players must convincingly be who they really are, whereas the other must try to pass as another gender. Turing describes his own variation as one where "a computer takes the place of player A," and so a literal reading would suggest that in his version the computer is not just pretending to be a human, but pretending to be a woman. It must pass as a she.

Other versions had it that player B could be either a man or a woman. It would seem a very different kind of game if only one player is faking, or if both are, or if neither of them are. Now that we give the computer a seat, we may have it pretending to be a woman along with a man pretending to be a woman, both trying to trick the interrogator into figuring out which is a man and which is a woman. Or perhaps a computer pretending to be a man pretending to be a woman, along with a man pretending to be a woman, or even a computer pretending to be a woman pretending to be a man pretending to be a woman! In the real world, of course, we already have all of the above.

"The Imitation Game," Morten Tyldum's Oscar-winning 2014 film about Turing, reminds us that the mathematician himself also had to "pass" — in his case as straight man in a society that criminalized homosexuality. Upon discovery that he was not what he appeared to be, he was forced to undergo horrific medical treatments known as "chemical castration." Ultimately the physical and emotional pain was too great and he committed suicide. The episode was grotesque tribute to a man whose contribution to defeating Hitler's military was still at that time a state secret. Turing was only recently given posthumous pardon, but the tens of thousands of other British men sentenced under similar laws have not.

One notes the sour ironic correspondence between asking an A.I. to "pass" the test in order to qualify as intelligent — to "pass" as a human intelligence — with Turing's own need to hide his homosexuality and to "pass" as a straight man. The demands of both bluffs are unnecessary and profoundly unfair.

Passing as a person, as a white or black person, or as a man or woman, for example, comes down to what others see and interpret. Because everyone else is already willing to read others according to conventional cues (of race, sex, gender, species, etc.) the complicity between whoever (or whatever) is passing and those among which he or she or it performs is what allows passing to succeed. Whether or not an A.I. is trying to pass as a human or is merely in drag as a human is another matter. Is the ruse all just a game or, as for some people who are compelled to pass in their daily lives, an essential camouflage? Either way, "passing" may say more about the audience than about the performers.

We would do better to presume that in our universe, "thinking" is much more diverse, even alien, than our own particular case. The real philosophical lessons of A.I. will have less to do with humans teaching machines how to think than with machines teaching humans a fuller and truer range of what thinking can be (and for that matter, what being human can be).

THAT WE WOULD wish to define the very existence of A.I. in relation to its ability to mimic how humans think that humans think will be looked back upon as a weird sort of speciesism. The legacy of that conceit helped to steer some older A.I. research down disappointingly fruitless paths, hoping to recreate human minds from available parts. It just doesn't work that way. Contemporary A.I. research suggests instead that the threshold by which any particular arrangement of matter can be said to be "intelligent" doesn't have much to do with how it reflects humanness back at us. As Stuart Russell and Peter Norvig (now director of research at Google) suggest in their essential A.I. textbook, biomorphic imitation is not how we design complex technology. Airplanes don't fly like birds fly, and we certainly don't try to trick birds into thinking that airplanes are birds in order to test whether those planes "really" are flying machines. Why do it for A.I. then? Today's serious A.I. research does not focus on the Turing Test as an objective criterion of success, and yet in our popular culture of A.I., the test's anthropocentrism holds such durable conceptual importance. Like the animals who talk like teenagers in a Disney movie, other minds are conceivable mostly by way of puerile ventriloquism.

One could argue that the anthropomorphic precondition for A.I. is a "pre-Copernican" attitude.

Where is the real injury in this? If we want everyday A.I. to be congenial in a humane sort of way, so what? The answer is that we have much to gain from a more sincere and disenchanted relationship to synthetic intelligences, and much to lose by keeping illusions on life support. Some philosophers write about the possible ethical "rights" of A.I. as sentient entities, but that's not my point here. Rather, the truer perspective is also the better one for us as thinking technical creatures.

Musk, Gates and Hawking made headlines by speaking to the dangers that A.I. may pose. Their points are important, but I fear were largely misunderstood by many readers. Relying on efforts to program A.I. not to "harm humans" (inspired by on Isaac Asimov's "three laws" of robotics from 1942) makes sense only when an A.I. knows what humans are and what harming them might mean. There are many ways that an A.I. might harm us that that have nothing to do with its malevolence toward us, and chief among these is exactly following our well-meaning instructions to an idiotic and catastrophic extreme. Instead of mechanical failure or a transgression of moral code, the A.I. may pose an existential risk because it is both powerfully intelligent and disinterested in humans. To the extent that we recognize A.I. by its anthropomorphic qualities, or presume its preoccupation with us, we are vulnerable to those eventualities.

Whether or not "hard A.I." ever appears, the harm is also in the loss of all that we prevent ourselves from discovering and understanding when we insist on protecting beliefs we know to be false. In the 1950 essay, Turing offers several rebuttals to his speculative A.I., including a striking comparison with earlier objections to Copernican astronomy. Copernican traumas that abolish the false centrality and absolute specialness of human thought and species-being are priceless accomplishments. They allow for human culture based on how the world actually is more than on how it appears to us from our limited vantage point. Turing referred to these as "theological objections," but one could argue that the anthropomorphic precondition for A.I. is a "pre-Copernican" attitude as well, however secular it may appear. The advent of robust inhuman A.I. may let us achieve another disenchantment, one that should enable a more reality-based understanding of ourselves, our situation, and a fuller and more complex understanding of what "intelligence" is and is not. From there we can hopefully make our world with a greater confidence that our models are good approximations of what's out there (always a helpful thing.)

Lastly, the harm is in perpetuating a relationship to technology that has brought us to the precipice of a Sixth Great Extinction. Arguably the Anthropocene itself is due less to technology run amok than to the humanist legacy that understands the world as having been given for our needs and created in our image. We hear this in the words of thought leaders who evangelize the superiority of a world where machines are subservient to the needs and wishes of humanity. If you think so, Google "pig decapitating machine" (actually, just don't) and then let's talk about inventing worlds in which machines are wholly subservient to humans' wishes.

One wonders whether it is only from a society that once gave theological and legislative comfort to chattel slavery that this particular affirmation could still be offered in 2015 with such satisfied naïveté? This is the sentiment — this philosophy of technology exactly — that is the basic algorithm of the Anthropocenic predicament, and consenting to it would also foreclose adequate encounters with A.I. It is time to move on. This pretentious folklore is too expensive.

BENJAMIN H. BRATTON (@bratton) is an associate professor of visual arts at the University of California, San Diego. His next book, "The Stack: On Software and Sovereignty," will be published this fall by the MIT

How I Learned to Stop Worrying and Love A.I.

OPINION | BY ROBERT A. BURTON | SEPT. 21, 2015

THE DISTINCTION BETWEEN man and machine is under siege. The technology wizard Ray Kurzweil speaks with casual confidence of achieving electromagnetic immortality with our once-human selves eternally etched onto universal servers. For me, the possibility that machines will acquire the equivalent of human feelings and emotions is pure fantasy. And yet, as a neurologist, I cannot ignore advancing machine intelligence's implications about the human mind.

To begin, think back to IBM's Deep Blue defeat of Garry Kasparov in 1997. One pivotal move that shifted the match in favor of Deep Blue prompted Kasparov to accuse IBM of human intervention. In so doing, he highlighted the essential cognitive dissonance that we will face as machines get smarter.

We know what it means to understand something because we experience the sensation of understanding. Machines don't.

Kasparov couldn't believe that he had been beaten by a computer because he felt the play was a sign of superior intelligence. But he was wrong — years later it was revealed by Deep Blue's co-creator that the triumphant move had been a result of a software bug. When presented with several options, Deep Blue could not make a definitive decision, so made a random move that rattled Kasparov.

Uncovering the so-called biology of creativity is big business. FMRI scan aficionados tell us which brain areas light up when someone has a novel idea. Brain wave experts propose electrical patterns specific to originality. Even if these observations pan out, they cannot tell us how to interpret a brilliant chess move arising out of a software glitch. If we are forced to expand our notion of creativity to include random electrical firings, what does that tell us about our highly touted imaginative superiority over a mindless machine?

For Kasparov, Deep Blue was an enigmatic black box, his opinions shaped by his biases as to what constitutes human versus machine intelligence. He's not alone. We have a strong personal sense of how humans think because we experience thoughts. We know what it means to understand something because we experience the sensation of understanding. This sense of understanding requires both consciousness and awareness of one's thoughts. We cannot conceive of understanding without consciousness.

What is overlooked in this equation is the quality or accuracy of the actual decision. A standard move by a chess player is evidence of understanding, but a superior move by an inanimate collection of wires and transistors is considered rote machine learning, not understanding. To put this in perspective, imagine a self-proclaimed chess novice making the same pivotal move as Deep Blue. I doubt that any of us would believe that she didn't know anything about chess.

Yet neuroscience is revealing that understanding isn't a result of conscious deliberation. From the hunch to the "aha," various degrees of the feeling of knowing are involuntary mental sensations that arise from subliminal brain mechanisms. They are the brain's way of telling us the likelihood that a subliminal thought is correct. More akin to bodily sensations than emotions, they can occur spontaneously, with certain psychoactive drugs and with direct brain stimulation in the absence of any conscious thought. We can't think up an aha — the ultimate sense of understanding. It just happens to us in the same way that we experience love and surprise.

Conversely, we can know things without any sense of knowing (as in the classic example of blindsight, where patients with cortical blindness can point out in which visual field a light is flashing even when they consciously see nothing and are entirely unaware of this knowledge).

If we accept that the feeling of understanding is an involuntary sensation that machines don't experience, you would think that we would stop worrying about what machines "understand." Not so. In 1980 the philosopher John Searle introduced the Chinese Room argument to show that it is impossible for digital computers to understand language or think. His 1999 summary of the argument goes as follows:

> *Imagine a native English speaker who knows no Chinese locked in a room full of boxes of Chinese symbols (a database) together with a book of instructions for manipulating the symbols (the program). Imagine that people outside the room send in other Chinese symbols which, unknown to the person in the room, are questions in Chinese (the input). And imagine that by following the instructions in the program the man in the room is able to pass out Chinese symbols which are correct answers to the questions (the output). The program enables the person in the room to pass the Turing Test for understanding Chinese but he does not understand a word of Chinese.*

Back in 1980, when we knew little about the brain and artificial intelligence hadn't yet flexed much practical muscle, the argument felt reasonable; absent the ability to understand, you wouldn't expect A.I. to make sophisticated decisions that are the equivalent of smart human thought. Thirty-five years later, though, the argument seems outdated. At bottom, it is a convoluted way of saying that machines don't have consciousness and feelings. Denying machine understanding tells us nothing about the potential limits of machine intelligence. Even so, according to the Stanford Encyclopedia of Philosophy, the Chinese Room argument remains the most widely discussed philosophical argument in cognitive science since the Turing Test.

It's as though our self-proclaimed position of superiority and uniqueness is constantly threatened, and we seem constitutionally compelled to compare ourselves to all other potentially thinking entities. A few hundred years ago, Descartes assumed that animals were automatons. Now we know that crows use tools and chimpanzees wage territorial war. Still, we aren't worried about crow and chimpanzee takeover of our planet, or that they are going to replace us as the highest life form on earth. But machines, well that's a different story.

TO HIS CREDIT, Kasparov saw the future. As the story goes, his close friends tried to console him for his loss by arguing that the computer had enormously greater computational power than the human brain, but did not understand chess. Kasparov's prescient response, referring to the vast amount of information the computer had processed: "More quantity creates better quality."

Most of us now know this to be true in our own lives. As a practicing neurologist, I took great pride in my clinical reservoir of obscure information. Now, any hand-held device with a modicum of memory has a greater and more accurate database. And it isn't just neurology. I have had a lifelong fascination with poker, and have managed a reasonable skill set based on practice, study and a bit of math. For me, the pleasure of the game is figuring out what an opponent has, what a bet means, when he's bluffing. In essence I have loved neurology and poker because they allow me to use my wits. No longer.

In the last several years, a poker-playing program (Cepheus) developed by the computer science department at the University of Alberta has consistently outplayed the world's best heads up limit hold 'em players. What makes this conquest so intriguing is that the computer isn't programmed in advance to play in any particular style or have any knowledge of the intricacies of poker theory. Instead it is an artificial neural network with a huge memory capacity (4000 terabytes). It plays and records the outcome of millions of trial and error simulations, eventually learning the optimal strategy for any given situation. It does so without any knowledge of the game or its opponent, or any of the subtleties that inform the best human players. It is completely in the dark as to why it does anything. (If you want, you can test your skills against the program at poker.srv.ualberta.ca.)

So if we are to accept reality, and acknowledge this sort of relative superiority in machines, how should we adapt? I like the perspective of a young friend of mine, a top flight professional hold 'em player, who has spent considerable time playing (but rarely winning) against Cepheus. He is hoping to improve his game by observing and unraveling the presumed reasons behind the computer's often counterintuitive plays. He doesn't care whether or not Cepheus understands anything about the game of poker. "Hey, I'm practical, not a philosopher. If it knows something that I don't, I'm all for learning it."

Rather than burden ourselves with biological biases as to what constitutes understanding, let me suggest adopting a new taxonomy. Let's give machines the status of a separate species with a distinctly different type of intellect — one that is superior in data crunching but is devoid of emotional reasoning. Not better, not worse, just different. No more condescension based on animistic beliefs. No more machine worship based on one's love of technology. Let's avoid using words like thinking and understanding when talking about machine intelligence; they add nothing to our understanding of their understanding (see what I mean?). We are slowly learning the myriad ways that animals and plants exhibit their own forms of intelligence; the same criteria should apply to machines.

The division is straightforward. For data that can be quantified, wisdom will become collective, not personal. We will ask our smart machines to tell us which will be the best treatment for an illness, the best move for a chess match or poker game, the optimal rush hour traffic flow, the likelihood of climate change. We cannot compete at this level.

The ultimate value added of human thought will lie in our ability to contemplate the non-quantifiable. Emotions, feelings and intentions — the stuff of being human — don't lend themselves to precise descriptions and calculations. Machines cannot and will not be able to tell us the best immigration policies, whether or not to proceed with gene therapy, or whether or not gun control is in our best interest. Computer modeling can show us how subtle biases can lead to overt racism and bigotry but cannot factor in the flood of feelings one experiences when looking at a photograph of a lynching.

Most of this seems too obvious for words. We have emotional intelligence; machines don't. Rather than fretting over what sources of pride machines will take from us, we should focus on those areas where man alone can make a difference.

In all fairness, this essay contains a long-festering personal agenda. My real concern is that, in keeping with our growing obsession with creating and using smart machines, we are on the way to losing the cognitive skills that won't be replaced by machines. Witness the decline in university enrollment in the humanities, the demise of the literary novel and the seeming obsession with information over contemplation. Of course nothing is black or white. Trends are in the eye of the beholder.

I confess to a bias for those minds that rely on scientific evidence and critical reasoning for those questions that can be answered empirically while simultaneously retaining a deep appreciation for the inexplicable, mysterious and emotionally complex — the indescribable yet palpable messiness that constitutes a life. For the latter, our value added isn't in any specific answer, but in the deeply considered question. In the end, it will be the quality of the questions that will be the measure of a man.

ROBERT A. BURTON, a former chief of neurology at the University of California, San Francisco Medical Center at Mt. Zion, is the author of "On Being Certain: Believing You Are Right Even When You're Not," and "A Skeptic's Guide to the Mind: What Neuroscience Can and Cannot Tell Us About Ourselves."

It's Westworld. What's Wrong With Cruelty to Robots?

OPINION | BY PAUL BLOOM AND SAM HARRIS | APRIL 23, 2018

SUPPOSE WE HAD ROBOTS perfectly identical to men, women and children and we were permitted by law to interact with them in any way we pleased. How would you treat them?

That is the premise of "Westworld," the popular HBO series that opened its second season Sunday night. And, plot twists of Season 2 aside, it raises a fundamental ethical question we humans in the not-so-distant future are likely to face.

Based on the 1973 film, "Westworld" depicts a futuristic playground modeled after the Wild West, where the characters — bartenders, prostitutes, sheriffs, bandits — are robotic "hosts," programmed to interact as naturally as possible with their human guests. These intelligent machines look and act exactly like people. Indeed, viewers are often confused or misled about who is a host and who is a person.

The guests can behave however they please. Some assume heroic roles, but others choose to act out their darkest impulses, participating in torture, rape and murder — including the murder of robots that are indistinguishable from human children. The hosts have been designed so that they can't harm the guests; so these are acts of pure sadism, without risk of reprisal.

It's hardly a spoiler to say that things go wrong for the humans in "Westworld." But we are interested here in the show's premise — and what our reaction as viewers to these lifelike robots suggests about human nature and the future of technology.

The biggest concern is that we might one day create conscious machines: sentient beings with beliefs, desires and, most morally pressing, the capacity to suffer. Nothing seems to be stopping us from doing this. Philosophers and scientists remain uncertain about how consciousness emerges from the material world, but few doubt that it does. This suggests that the creation of conscious machines is possible.

Suppose, as many philosophers and scientists believe, that consciousness arises in a sufficiently complex system that processes information. There is no reason to think that such a system need be made of meat. Conscious minds are most likely platform-independent — ultimately the product of the right software. It seems only a matter of time before we either emulate the workings of the human brain in our computers or build conscious minds of another sort.

And even if one believes that only biological systems can be conscious, this development, too, lies within our reach — perhaps through a combination of artificial intelligence and genetic engineering. Indeed, in "Westworld," it's hinted that the hosts are partly biological. We certainly see them bleed.

If we did create conscious beings, conventional morality tells us that it would be wrong to harm them — precisely to the degree that they are conscious, and can suffer or be deprived of happiness. Just as it would be wrong to breed animals for the sake of torturing them, or to have children only to enslave them, it would be wrong to mistreat the conscious machines of the future.

But how will we know if our machines become conscious? Descartes argued that one's own consciousness is beyond any possibility of doubt. In the case of others, we're never absolutely sure. Many of us have entertained, if only for a moment, the idea that everyone else might be a zombie: laughing, crying, complaining, rejoicing, but with no one home. Perhaps scientists will eventually discover the signature of consciousness, and then we will be able to test for it in our robots, as well as in animals and one another. But it is certain that we will build machines that seem conscious long before we arrive at that point.

Anything that looks and acts like the hosts on "Westworld" will appear conscious to us, whether or not we understand how consciousness emerges in physical systems. Indeed, experiments with AI and robotics have already shown how quick we are to attribute feelings to machines that look and behave like independent agents. Multiply that temptation to anthropomorphize a thousandfold: Think not of a machine with visible wires, cartoonish eyes and a voice that sounds like Siri but of a beautiful stranger who engages you in intelligent conversation and who may be more aware of your emotions than your spouse or best friends ever were. It would be irresistible to see this creature as a person, whatever your philosophical views and regardless of what its creators told you about how it was built.

This is where actually watching "Westworld" matters. The pleasure of entertainment aside, the makers of the series have produced a powerful work of philosophy. It's one thing to sit in a seminar and argue about what it would mean, morally, if robots were conscious. It's quite another to witness the torments of such creatures, as portrayed by actors such as Evan Rachel Wood and Thandie Newton. You may still raise the question intellectually, but in your heart and your gut, you already know the answer.

Watching the show, you also discover how you feel about the people who rape, torture and kill these robots. We have no idea how many people would actually behave this way in a place like Westworld (the show implies that there's no shortage of such customers), but there is something repugnant about those who do. In this scenario, the robot hosts are the most human and the humans who abuse them are monsters.

Kant had odd views about animals, seeing them as mere things, devoid of moral value, but he insisted on their proper treatment because of the implications for how we treat one another: "For he who is cruel to animals becomes hard also in his dealings with men." We could surely say the same for the treatment of lifelike robots. Even if we could be certain that they weren't conscious and couldn't really suffer, their torture would very likely harm the torturer and, ultimately, the other people in his life.

This may seem like an extreme version of the worry that many have about violent video games. It has long been speculated that enacting violence in a virtual world desensitizes people to violence in the real one. The evidence for such an effect turns out to be weak. In fact, as video games have become increasingly realistic, the rate of violent crime has dropped.

But the prospect of building a place like "Westworld" is much more troubling, because the experience of harming a host isn't merely similar to that of harming a person; it's identical. We have no idea what repeatedly indulging such fantasies would do to us, ethically or psychologically — but there seems little reason to think that it would be good.

The issues here extend beyond sadism. Machines are created to improve the lives of human beings, and one of the attractions of advanced AI is the prospect of robot maids, butlers and chauffeurs (also known as self-driving cars). This is all fine with the sorts of machines we currently have, but as AI improves, we run a moral risk.

After all, if we do manage to create machines as smart as or smarter than we are — and, more important, machines that can feel — it's hardly clear that it would be ethical for us to use them to do our bidding, even if they were programmed to enjoy such drudgery. The notion of genetically engineering a race of willing slaves is a standard trope of science fiction, wherein humankind is revealed to have done something terrible. Why would the production of sentient robot slaves be any different?

For the first time in our history, then, we run the risk of building machines that only monsters would use as they please.

PAUL BLOOM is a professor of psychology at Yale and the author of "Against Empathy: The Case for Rational Compassion." **SAM HARRIS** is a neuroscientist, the author of "Waking Up: A Guide to Spirituality Without Religion," and the host of the "Waking Up Podcast."

Glossary

algorithm A straightforward rule that computers use to solve sets of problems.

artificial neural network Computing systems capable of learning autonomously from examples; resembles the neural networks of animal brains.

autonomous Describes the ability to act independently.

big data Data sets that are too large and complex for traditional data-processing software to manage.

black box Describes a situation in which inputs (data) and outputs (answers) are visible, but the way a program comes up with answers is unknown.

chatbot An artificial intelligence that is capable of having a vocal or textual conversation.

cognitive Describes the process of gaining knowledge and understanding from thought and sensory experience.

deep learning A machine's ability to simulate human thought by using neural networks to process data in such a way that it can make connections autonomously.

existential threat The theory that advanced A.I. will pose a threat to the existence of humanity or other life on the planet.

facial recognition A technology that can identify an individual from an image or video.

intelligence explosion The idea that artificial intelligence may become capable of improving itself autonomously, leading to a superintelligent A.I.

intelligent agent An autonomous entity that is capable of observing and acting on its environment to achieve its goals.

machine intelligence A synonym for artificial intelligence; a machine that can think.

machine learning In computer science, the use of statistical techniques to teach programs to use data on their own to improve at performing tasks.

machine perception A computer system's ability to perceive and interpret data.

moral Describes principles of right or wrong actions and goodness or badness.

pattern recognition An A.I.'s ability to recognize patterns in data.

predictive policing The practice of using data to predict criminal activity.

singularity The theory that the development of strong A.I. will inaugurate unprecedented and unpredictable advances in technology that will radically alter human civilizations.

speech recognition Technology that allows computers to recognize speech and translate it into text.

superintelligence An intelligence that surpasses that of even the most intelligent humans.

Turing test Developed by Alan Turing, a test to determine if a machine possesses human-like intelligence: a human has a conversation with a machine. If the human cannot tell he or she is speaking with a machine, the machine passes the test.

Media Literacy Terms

"Media literacy" refers to the ability to access, understand, critically assess and create media. The following terms are important components of media literacy, and they will help you critically engage with the articles in this title.

angle The aspect of a news story on which a journalist focuses and develops.

attribution The method by which a source is identified or by which facts and information are assigned to the person who provided them.

balance Principle of journalism that both perspectives of an argument should be presented in a fair way.

chronological order Method of writing a story presenting the details of the story in the order in which they occurred.

column A type of story that is a regular feature, often on a recurring topic, written by the same journalist, generally known as a columnist.

commentary Type of story that is an expression of opinion on recent events by a journalist generally known as a commentator.

credibility The quality of being trustworthy and believable, said of a journalistic source.

critical review Type of story that describes an event or work of art, such as a theater performance, film, concert, book, restaurant, radio or television program, exhibition or musical piece, and offers critical assessment of its quality and reception.

editorial Article of opinion or interpretation.

feature story Article designed to entertain as well as to inform.

headline Type, usually 18 point or larger, used to introduce a story.

human interest story Type of story that focuses on individuals and how events or issues affect their lives, generally offering a sense of relatability to the reader.

impartiality Principle of journalism that a story should not reflect a journalist's bias and should contain balance.

intention The motive or reason behind something, such as the publication of a news story.

interview story Type of story in which the facts are gathered primarily by interviewing another person or persons.

motive The reason behind something, such as the publication of a news story or a source's perspective on an issue.

news story An article or style of expository writing that reports news, generally in a straightforward fashion and without editorial comment.

op-ed An opinion piece that reflects a prominent individual's opinion on a topic of interest.

paraphrase The summary of an individual's words, with attribution, rather than a direct quotation of their exact words.

quotation The use of an individual's exact words indicated by the use of quotation marks and proper attribution.

reliability The quality of being dependable and accurate, said of a journalistic source.

rhetorical device Technique in writing intending to persuade the reader or communicate a message from a certain perspective.

source The origin of the information reported in journalism.

tone A manner of expression in writing or speech.

Media Literacy Questions

1. What is the intention of the article "A Fight to Win the Future: Computers vs. Humans" (on page 16)? How effectively does it achieve its intended purpose?

2. "Google's A.I. Program Rattles Chinese Go Master as It Wins Match" (on page 39) is an example of a feature story. What is the purpose of a feature story? Does this article achieve that purpose?

3. Does Claire Cain Miller demonstrate the journalistic principle of impartiality in her article "Will You Lose Your Job to a Robot? Silicon Valley Is Split" (on page 60)? If so, how? If not, how could she have made her article more impartial?

4. Identify each of the sources in "Google Promises Its A.I. Will Not Be Used for Weapons" (on page 131) as a primary or a secondary source. Evaluate the reliability and credibility of each source. How does your evaluation of each source change your perspective on this article?

5. What type of story is "Leave A.I. Alone" (on page 167)? Can you identify another article in this collection that is the same type of story? What elements helped you come to your conclusion?

6. What is the intention of the article "When the Robot Doesn't See Dark Skin" (on page 140)? How effectively does the piece achieve its purpose?

7. The article "The Future of Moral Machines" (on page 174) is an example of an op-ed. Identify how Colin Allen's attitude and tone help convey his opinion on the topic.

8. "Inside China's Dystopian Dreams: A.I., Shame and Lots of Cameras" (on page 151) features photographs. What do these photographs add to the article?

9. Identify the various sources cited in the article "Mark Zuckerberg, Elon Musk and the Feud Over Killer Robots" (on page 121). How does Cade Metz attribute information to each of these sources in his article? How effective are Metz's attributions in helping the reader identify his sources?

10. "Busting the Myths About A.I. Invading Our Lives" (on page 42) is an example of an interview. What are the benefits of providing readers with direct quotes of an interviewed subject's speech? Is the subject of an interview always a reliable source?

11. Analyze the authors' reporting in "A.I. Will Transform the Economy. But How Much, and How Soon?" (on page 91) and "Will Robots Take Our Children's Jobs?" (on page 95). Do you think one journalist is more balanced in their reporting than the other? If so, why do you think so?

12. Compare the headlines of "How to Regulate Artificial Intelligence" (on page 164) and "Leave A.I. Alone" (on page 167). Which is a more compelling headline, and why? How could the less compelling headline be changed to better draw the reader's interest?

Citations

All citations in this list are formatted according to the Modern Language Association's (MLA) style guide.

BOOK CITATION

THE NEW YORK TIMES EDITORIAL STAFF. *Artificial Intelligence.* New York: New York Times Educational Publishing, 2019.

ARTICLE CITATIONS

ALLEN, COLIN. "The Future of Moral Machines." *The New York Times*, 25 Dec. 2011, opinionator.blogs.nytimes.com/2011/12/25/the-future-of-moral-machines/.

BLOOM, PAUL, AND SAM HARRIS. "It's Westworld. What's Wrong With Cruelty to Robots?" *The New York Times*, 23 Apr. 2018, www.nytimes.com/2018/04/23/opinion/westworld-conscious-robots-morality.html?rref=collection/column/the-stone.

BRATTON, BENJAMIN H. "Outing A.I.: Beyond the Turing Test." *The New York Times*, 23 Feb. 2015, opinionator.blogs.nytimes.com/2015/02/23/outing-a-i-beyond-the-turing-test/?rref=collection/column/the-stone.

BROOKS, DAVID. "Our Machine Masters." *The New York Times*, 31 Oct. 2014, www.nytimes.com/2014/10/31/opinion/david-brooks-our-machine-masters.html.

BUOLAMWINI, JOY. "When the Robot Doesn't See Dark Skin." *The New York Times*, 21 June 2018, www.nytimes.com/2018/06/21/opinion/facial-analysis-technology-bias.html.

BURT, ANDREW. "Leave A.I. Alone." *The New York Times*, 4 Jan. 2018, www.nytimes.com/2018/01/04/opinion/leave-artificial-intelligence.html.

BURTON, ROBERT A. "How I Learned to Stop Worrying and Love A.I." *The New York Times*, 21 Sept. 2015, opinionator.blogs.nytimes.com/2015/09/21/how-i-learned-to-stop-worrying-and-love-a-i/?rref=collection/column/the-stone.

CARR, NICHOLAS. "These Are Not the Robots We Were Promised." *The New*

York Times, 9 Sept. 2017, www.nytimes.com/2017/09/09/opinion/sunday/household-robots-alexa-homepod.html.

CHOKSHI, NIRAJ. "Most Americans See Artificial Intelligence as a Threat to Jobs (Just Not Theirs)." *The New York Times*, 6 Mar. 2018, www.nytimes.com/2018/03/06/us/artificial-intelligence-jobs.html.

CIXIN, LIU. "The Robot Revolution Will Be the Quietest One." *The New York Times*, 21 Dec. 2017, www.nytimes.com/2016/12/07/opinion/the-robot-revolution-will-be-the-quietest-one.html.

DE AENLLE, CONRAD. "A.I. Has Arrived in Investing. Humans Are Still Dominating." *The New York Times*, 12 Jan. 2018, www.nytimes.com/2018/01/12/business/ai-investing-humans-dominating.html.

ETZIONI, OREN. "How to Regulate Artificial Intelligence." *The New York Times*, 2 Sept. 2017, www.nytimes.com/2017/09/01/opinion/artificial-intelligence-regulations-rules.html.

HAFNER, KATIE. "Still a Long Way From Checkmate." *The New York Times*, 28 Dec. 2000, www.nytimes.com/2000/12/28/technology/still-a-long-way-from-checkmate.html.

KERSTETTER, JIM. "The Limits of A.I." *The New York Times*, 16 June 2017, www.nytimes.com/2017/06/16/technology/facebook-the-limits-of-ai.html.

LEE, KAI-FU. "The Real Threat of Artificial Intelligence." *The New York Times*, 24 June 2017, www.nytimes.com/2017/06/24/opinion/sunday/artificial-intelligence-economic-inequality.html.

LI, FEI-FEI. "How to Make A.I. That's Good for People." *The New York Times*, 8 Mar. 2018, www.nytimes.com/2018/03/07/opinion/artificial-intelligence-human.html.

LOHR, STEVE. "A.I. Is Doing Legal Work. But It Won't Replace Lawyers, Yet." *The New York Times*, 19 Mar. 2017, www.nytimes.com/2017/03/19/technology/lawyers-artificial-intelligence.html.

LOHR, STEVE. "A.I. Will Transform the Economy. But How Much, and How Soon?" *The New York Times*, 30 Nov. 2017, www.nytimes.com/2017/11/30/technology/ai-will-transform-the-economy-but-how-much-and-how-soon.html.

MALCOMSON, SCOTT. "Why Silicon Valley Shouldn't Work With the Pentagon." *The New York Times*, 19 Apr. 2018, www.nytimes.com/2018/04/19/opinion/silicon-valley-military-contract.html.

MARKOFF, JOHN. "Artificial Intelligence Is Far From Matching Humans, Panel Says." *The New York Times*, 21 Dec. 2017, www.nytimes.com/2016/05/26/technology/artificial-intelligence-is-far-from-matching-humans-panel-says.html.

MARKOFF, JOHN. "As Artificial Intelligence Evolves, So Does Its Criminal Potential." *The New York Times*, 21 Dec. 2017, www.nytimes.com/2016/10/24/technology/artificial-intelligence-evolves-with-its-criminal-potential.html.

MARKOFF, JOHN. "The End of Lawyers? Not So Fast." *The New York Times*, 4 Jan. 2016, bits.blogs.nytimes.com/2016/01/04/the-end-of-work-not-so-fast/.

MARKOFF, JOHN. "A Fight to Win the Future: Computers vs. Humans." *The New York Times*, 14 Feb. 2011, www.nytimes.com/2011/02/15/science/15essay.html.

MARKOFF, JOHN. "How Tech Giants Are Devising Real Ethics for Artificial Intelligence." *The New York Times*, 21 Dec. 2017, www.nytimes.com/2016/09/02/technology/artificial-intelligence-ethics.html.

MARKOFF, JOHN. "Scientists Worry Machines May Outsmart Man." *The New York Times*, 25 July 2009, www.nytimes.com/2009/07/26/science/26robot.html.

MARKOFF, JOHN. "Software Is Smart Enough for SAT, but Still Far From Intelligent." *The New York Times*, 20 Sept. 2015, www.nytimes.com/2015/09/21/technology/personaltech/software-is-smart-enough-for-sat-but-still-far-from-intelligent.html.

MASON, ELISABETH A. "A.I. and Big Data Could Power a New War on Poverty." *The New York Times*, 1 Jan. 2018, www.nytimes.com/2018/01/01/opinion/ai-and-big-data-could-power-a-new-war-on-poverty.html.

METZ, CADE. "Busting the Myths About A.I. Invading Our Lives." *The New York Times*, 13 Dec. 2017, www.nytimes.com/2017/12/13/technology/personaltech/busting-myths-ai.html.

METZ, CADE. "Mark Zuckerberg, Elon Musk and the Feud Over Killer Robots." *The New York Times*, 9 June 2018, www.nytimes.com/2018/06/09/technology/elon-musk-mark-zuckerberg-artificial-intelligence.html.

MILLER, CLAIRE CAIN. "Will You Lose Your Job to a Robot? Silicon Valley Is Split." *The New York Times*, 6 Aug. 2014, www.nytimes.com/2014/08/07/upshot/will-you-lose-your-job-to-a-robot-silicon-valley-is-split.html.

MOZUR, PAUL. "Google's A.I. Program Rattles Chinese Go Master as It Wins Match." *The New York Times*, 25 May 2017, www.nytimes.com/2017/05/25/business/google-alphago-defeats-go-ke-jie-again.html.

MOZUR, PAUL. "Inside China's Dystopian Dreams: A.I., Shame and Lots of Cameras." *The New York Times*, 8 July 2018, www.nytimes.com/2018/07/08/business/china-surveillance-technology.html.

THE NEW YORK TIMES. "How Artificial Intelligence Is Edging Its Way Into Our Lives." *The New York Times*, 12 Feb. 2018, www.nytimes.com/2018/02/12/technology/artificial-intelligence-new-work-summit.html.

THE NEW YORK TIMES. "Of Lawyers and Robots." *The New York Times*, 3 Apr. 2017, www.nytimes.com/2017/04/03/opinion/of-lawyers-and-robots.html.

THE NEW YORK TIMES. "A Robot for a Lawyer?" *The New York Times*, 7 Apr. 2017, www.nytimes.com/2017/04/07/opinion/a-robot-for-a-lawyer.html.

PANDE, VIJAY. "Artificial Intelligence's 'Black Box' Is Nothing to Fear." *The New York Times*, 25 Jan. 2018, www.nytimes.com/2018/01/25/opinion/artificial-intelligence-black-box.html.

PRICE, HUW. "Cambridge, Cabs and Copenhagen: My Route to Existential Risk." *The New York Times*, 27 Jan. 2013, opinionator.blogs.nytimes.com/2013/01/27/cambridge-cabs-and-copenhagen-my-route-to-existential-risk/?rref=collection/column/the-stone.

ROOSE, KEVIN. "Here Come the Fake Videos, Too." *The New York Times*, 5 Mar. 2018, www.nytimes.com/2018/03/04/technology/fake-videos-deepfakes.html.

ROSENTHAL, ELISABETH. "Can a Computer Replace Your Doctor?" *The New York Times*, 21 Dec. 2017, www.nytimes.com/2014/09/21/sunday-review/high-tech-health-care-useful-to-a-point.html.

SCHNEIDER, SUSAN. "The Philosophy of 'Her'." *The New York Times*, 2 Mar. 2014, opinionator.blogs.nytimes.com/2014/03/02/the-philosophy-of-her/?rref=collection/column/the-stone.

VICTOR, DANIEL. "Elon Musk and Stephen Hawking Among Hundreds to Urge Ban on Military Robots." *The New York Times*, 21 Dec. 2017, www.nytimes.com/2015/07/28/technology/elon-musk-and-stephen-hawking-among-hundreds-to-urge-ban-on-military-robots.html.

WAKABAYASHI, DAISUKE. "Meet the People Who Train the Robots (to Do Their Own Jobs)." *The New York Times*, 28 Apr. 2017, www.nytimes.com/2017/04/28/technology/meet-the-people-who-train-the-robots-to-do-their-own-jobs.html.

WAKABAYASHI, DAISUKE, AND CADE METZ. "Google Promises Its A.I. Will Not Be Used for Weapons." *The New York Times*, 7 June 2018, www.nytimes.com/2018/06/07/technology/google-artificial-intelligence-weapons.html.

WILLIAMS, ALEX. "Will Robots Take Our Children's Jobs?" *The New York Times*, 11 Dec. 2017, www.nytimes.com/2017/12/11/style/robots-jobs-children.html.

WILLIAMS, BÄRÍ A. " 'Intelligent' Policing and My Innocent Children." *The New York Times*, 2 Dec. 2017, www.nytimes.com/2017/12/02/opinion/sunday/intelligent-policing-and-my-innocent-children.html.

Index

This book is current up until the time of printing. For the most up-to-date reporting, visit www.nytimes.com.